HORSETHIEF'S MOON

HORSETHIEF'S MOON

LAURAN PAINE

WHEELER
CHIVERS

This Large Print edition is published by Wheeler Publishing, Waterville, Maine, USA and by AudioGO Ltd, Bath, England.
Wheeler Publishing, a part of Gale, Cengage Learning.
The text of this Large Print edition is unabridged.
Other aspects of the book may vary from the original edition.
Set in 16 pt. Plantin.

LIBRARY OF CONGRESS CATALOGING-IN-PUBLICATION DATA

Paine, Lauran.
   Horsethief's moon / by Lauran Paine. — Large print ed.
     p. cm. (Wheeler publishing large print western)
   ISBN-13: 978-1-4104-3979-6 (pbk.)
   ISBN-10: 1-4104-3979-8 (pbk.)
   1. Large type books. I. Title.
PS3566.A34H68 2011
813'.54—dc22   2011017532

BRITISH LIBRARY CATALOGUING-IN-PUBLICATION DATA AVAILABLE

Published in 2011 in the U.S. by arrangement with Golden West Literary Agency.
Published in 2012 in the U.K. by arrangement with Golden West Literary Agency.

U.K. Hardcover: 978 1 445 83848 9 (Chivers Large Print)
U.K. Softcover: 978 1 445 83849 6 (Camden Large Print)

Printed in the United States of America
1 2 3 4 5 6 7 15 14 13 12 11

HORSETHIEF'S MOON

1
LONG GRASS VALLEY

The oldtime *ozuye we tawatas* used the bluff for a point of vantage, and during their sentinel-time some of them sat and chipped out arrowheads. The flakes, and even some of the old deer horns they had used to chip the stone, were still up there. Occasionally, people had even found perfectly good arrowheads, perhaps dropped or misplaced.

There had not been an Indian, Sioux or any other kind, up there now for years. It was a lonely, solitary place of old trees standing through interminable snows and sunblasts upon a flinty scurf of crumbly stone and soil, absolutely silent and lonely.

But the panorama from up there was magnificent. All of Long Grass Valley could be seen, and it ran for nearly eighty miles from east to west, and about half that many miles north and south. On a clear day the town of Cutler was visible, lying south and east about thirty, forty miles, and usually the days this time of year were flawless, the air like faint perfume from pinesap in the upland mountains and wild flowers, columbines and lupins, down in the foothills and out across the cow country.

Wyoming and Montana had dozens of these hidden highland plateaux with mountains ringing them. Hundreds of them in fact but accessibility kept many from being settled. The lack of towns mattered too. Down where Cutler stood the Long Grass creek and the Spur river met and mingled. Even in drought-times Cutler had never lacked for all the water it needed with enough left over to still fill both beds. Also, in the early days there had been a share of gold washed down there. That was, so folks said now, the reason Cutler had come to exist at all, but in fact an old Indian named Teats had once told Jeffrey Wayman's father there had always been a village there; that his grandfather had told him of that village and he had got it from *his* grandfather.

For a fact, it was common when digging graves out back of town at the cemetery, or while excavating for fir-log foundations under buildings in town, or around it, to turn up old bones, some white of animals, some darker of people. Also trinkets, even stone knives and skulls, many with dents in them, as well as arrowheads by the score, layer upon layer, so probably old Teats had been telling the truth.

Jeff Wayman's Mexican *remudero* had been bringing back horses off the bluffs one time and had come upon a surprisingly preserved burial shroud lashed high in a tree. They had all gone back up there a few days later to stare at it. Caloway Hamilton the rangeboss had chewed, spat amber, chewed some more and had finally said, "The last Sioux — let him rest in peace," and that sentiment had infected them all so they turned back to the downhill trail and did not go back to that particular place again, until one time Jeff came in from pot-hunting the farther mountains with an elk on his pack-mule and had passed beneath the tree. The old Sioux was still up there.

The Waymans had run horses against the cliff and ranging westerly ten miles along the tawny bluffs for two generations. They had made money supplying the army in the early days, and they had lost horses which had also supplied the Sioux those same years. Jeff's father had raised the price to the army to compensate for inadvertently supplying the Indians. In the end the army was still around needing horses and the Sioux were not. Wayman's Rafter W on an animal's left shoulder meant good horse-flesh. The old man had been a stickler for quality in a country and at a time when all most riders cared about was something wrapped in horsehide to get them there and get them back.

Jeff felt the same way, probably because his father had raised him believing only quality horseflesh was worth feeding. One thing the old man had said was certainly true: It did not take one bit more feed to keep a good horse going than it took to maintain a poor one.

Jeff's father had trailed through on his way back from Montana. Had in fact sat his horse atop that same cliff where the arrowhead-chips were still lying scattered, and had made up his mind on the spot he would own a part of Long Grass Valley, spend the balance of his life there and be buried there.

He had fulfilled that promise to the letter. He was buried out east of the massive log home and barn and sheds he had created, inside a picket fence alongside the 'breed woman named Bethany he had married, after a raid on a Sioux camp in search of stolen horses. She was buried there beside the old man. Jeff's mother and father. There had been a stillborn-daughter; she was also buried over there. Otherwise, Jeff was the only descendant and at thirty-six he had never married so it appeared Rafter W would end when Jeff ended.

That was what people said anyway, and in a place as isolated as Long Grass Valley people did not have much more to do, especially in the bleak winters of up-country Wyoming, than to specialise in the business of their neighbours. Even when a neighbour was someone they did not see more than perhaps once or twice a year — sometimes not even that often — because the ranches were widely scattered and the town of Cutler was even farther off.

It was a world of social order despite its vastness and the sparseness of its inhabitants. A very simple and effective morality existed. Killers were in turn killed; thieves, depending upon what they stole — horses or cattle — were hanged where apprehended, other varieties of thieves were given until nightfall to be out of the country, and it was common to make certain they got out. Otherwise, a lot of them dropped from sight forever, too.

But the people were neither bloodthirsty nor flint-hearted. The ones within decent distance of Cutler drove in every Sunday for church services. At the far places like

Rafter W they observed the Sabbath by loafing, usually anyway, and no one abided a liar.

The life was simple, rewarding, and usually hard. When Jeff took bands of horses down to the public corrals at Cutler several times a year, his riders cut loose in town, but that was expected. It was normal. Even so, they were for the most part not troublesome enough to get locked up. The town marshal down there, big, shock-headed Craig Stanton with fists like hams, rarely used a gun against rangemen. He rarely had to. As Caloway Hamilton once said, on a return-ride after an encounter with Marshal Stanton at the *Long Grass Saloon,* Craig Stanton was big enough to throw a saddle on and tough enough to chew spikes and spit rust.

Cal was fresh from experiencing some of that toughness, and Caloway Hamilton was not a small nor soft man. He hadn't lasted one full minute, and afterwards Marshal Stanton had dragged him to the jailhouse under the approving smiles of townsmen, but instead of locking Caloway up, Stanton had propped him in a chair, had lectured him and had kept pouring hot and bitter black coffee down Caloway until he was sober enough to sleep it off in an unlocked cell until morning, when Rafter W was ready to ride out.

But Jeff Wayman's men rarely rode down that far. Cutler was a long way from the bluffs. Many miles too far for a Saturday night outing, and rangeriders who could not stand being that far from a town did not stay long. As a matter of fact most of Jeff's riders seemed perfectly content to ride for an outfit which was so far away from the stageroad and the town. Occasionally, someone murmured darkly about this, but in Long Grass Valley there were others who probably preferred being inconspicuous, among the other bunkhouses and ranges, so the topic never got very much discussion.

If, as it was hinted, there were wanted men in Long Grass Valley, they must not have felt like practising their trade of robbery or murder of whatever it was they might be wanted for; Long Grass Valley was an orderly place, by and large, and when occasional instances of lawlessness occurred it was without exception the work of men who did not live nor work there. But even then those instances were very rare.

In Cutler, folks said there wasn't enough real money in all of Long Grass Valley to fill a Mexican hat. They said this was probably the main reason there was so little lawless-

13

ness. But that was to assume all outlaws ever looked for was money, which was not true. They also stole cattle and horses.

Craig Stanton, who had led a few posses out over the years since he'd been township lawman, had another, more trenchant observation about the lack of lawlessness.

He once told Jeff that he had yet to round up possemen at random from the countryside without having at least two good trackers among a band of men who could think exactly the way outlaws thought, when they were fleeing. That, he had said drily, made it worthwhile to take up a manhunt; and he had also said he had never once questioned how any of those men were so knowledgeable. All he had wanted to do upon those occasions was get his fugitives and get back to town. Without exception he had been successful.

Jeff had heard all the stories. He had heard tales of earlier times from his father and he was reasonably certain that in the ten years since his father had died and he had operated Rafter W, he had hired his share of men who had come in out of the surrounding mountains and forests to hire on, who worked hard and well without saying a single word about themselves.

Nor did he ask. Caloway was with him

14

one time, east along the brakes below the foothills looking for horses when they startled three men in a smokeless camp. The men had scattered like sage hens, leaving behind three Wells Fargo cotton bags about the size of those two-pound flour sacks riders packed along — empty.

Jeff would have stopped and Caloway shook his head. "You get down off that horse, Jeff, and go near that camp, and those fellers in the trees will kill you. Just look straight ahead, ride along with me now, and don't even turn your head and look up there . . . See them saddleboots? Empty! Maybe we come onto them unexpected but they took the Winchesters when they run . . . Just keep here beside me like we didn't see anything."

His father had told him as a young rider that men who minded their own business had a fair chance of dying in bed.

If was sound advice. In fact, it would always be sound advice.

Of the four men, including his rangeboss, who rode Rafter W range, not a one went horse-hunting, or worked the bands at the pole corrals, or loafed of a Sunday doing laundry at the creek, shaving, or playing cards in the old log bunkhouse, ever went without his shellbelt and gun.

15

Ordinary cowboys never wore weapons when at a working-ground or while doing routine range work. The belts were heavy and the guns made them heavier. They also got in the way and every time a man wanted to squat or sit, he had to shift the things; they were a plain nuisance — unless men had long ago learned to live with that, for whatever reason, and it was hard to imagine why men would tolerate the inconvenience unless they had one hell of a good reason for doing so.

Jeff seldom went armed, although like a good many rangemen, he carried a boot-knife; a hunting knife actually, kept scabbarded in a sheath sewn into the outside of his boot-upper, next to his leg. Not especially for self-protection but to slash ropes in an emergency, to swiftly alter bull calves or stud colts encountered on the range, or for slicing meat at a camp-ground, or whittling kindling. They were far superior to little pocket-knives.

It was a weapon only as a last resort. In a country where other men were very likely to be armed with sixguns, it was not in fact even a very good weapon.

Jeff, in his mid-thirties, a shade on the sundown-side of them in fact, had been packing a bootknife all his mature years and had never once drawn the thing in anger. His father had given it to him at the same time the old man had returned from Cheyenne one autumn with Jeff's first pair of boots.

The old man had presented it to him the same way he would have given his son a new hat or a leather vest; part of a man's necessary, everyday using equipment. How the custom had got started was anyone's guess, but back in the early days there had been French-Canadian *voyageurs,* trappers mostly, who had worn bootknives; in their trade a man skinned trapped critters all winter long. He had to carry a knife, and although he usually did so in a sheath on his belt, rangemen had begun carrying them in scabbards sewn inside the boots, a more handy place for someone who needed his belt for other things.

2
JOHN AND JASPER

In Long Grass Valley springtime usually arrived late. Northern Wyoming was close enough to Montana to share that area's weather patterns. Even with the advent of warmth in the winter-sun again, the days were rarely warm enough not for riders to need at least a sheep-pelt lined leather vest, and the nights required a lot more than that, usually a big dry-wood fire in a camp, or a popping iron stove in a bunkhouse.

When late spring rolled over into summer the days got warmer, but the nights rarely did; not until July and August as a rule. By then, the days were hot and that bothered men who were more accustomed to cold than heat.

Linton Foster, who had been riding Rafter W range for two years, said one time that just when a man's blood was thick enough to stand the cold, the damned summers came and he had to wait until about September for his blood to thin out, by which time it got cold again. He laughed about that, shaking his head. "No peace in this world, unless a man can get down along the Messican border. And down there they'll steal your boots while you're sleepin' at night, and cut your throat for an old saddle."

Jeff's *remudero* was a Mexican. Not a genuine one; he had been born in West Texas — what genuine Mexicans called a *"pocho"*. He had answered Lin Foster with a black-eyed smile which was not altogether amused.

"They'll do the same to you in Kansas or Nebraska. And at Dodge City they won't even wait for you to go to bed to cut your throat."

Lin smiled. He and the horse-wrangler were friends. "Luis, you ate a disagreeable cuss. And I didn't mean *all* Messicans anyway."

Luis Sanchez was in fact good-natured, tolerant, and violent in anger, a not-uncommon contradiction in *pochos,* or any other variety of Mexicans. He had shrugged thin shoulders by way of ending their moment of sparks. He was smaller than the others and pounds lighter, but on horseback he had more grace than any of them. He was one of those men who had been born to sit a saddle. He could think like a horse and rope like a tophand. He could 'doctor' animals with a sureness which was uncanny, and he had a knack for winnowing out the fear and temper in colts to be broken. He never went anywhere, not even to the breaking-corral to ride colts, without his ivory-handled sixgun.

He and Linton Foster team-roped when the bands were brought in for working and although there was an occasional sharp word, generally they teased each other like all the other men did.

Lin was tall and lean; at least six inches taller than Luis Sanchez, but that ivory-handled Colt was the best equaliser in the world, and tall men made easier targets.

Once on a slack Sunday they had set up slats to fire at from the rear porch of the bunkhouse. Luis Sanchez was the most accurate shot among them and he never smiled while he was shooting.

He was not as fast as Lin Foster. None of them were. But these were men who had matured in an environment where a fast draw seemed flashy, pretentious. They had lived as long as they had by concentrating on accuracy. There was not a poor shot among them, but that Sunday Jeff Wayman had been down at Cutler. He was not a particularly handy man with pistols although he was good enough with rifles or saddleguns. Not because he practised but because he had been hunting all his life and sooner or later a hunting man became proficient or he came back skunked.

The following Tuesday they went out all in a band to bring in thirty head. Jeff had an agreement with a buyer in Cutler for thirty Rafter W geldings, not under three and not over seven. But every one of them was riding a horse over seven when they left. Caloway had always averred a horse was like most men; he didn't get much sense until he was close to being smooth-mouthed.

They knew their range, knew in late springtime about where the bands would be. The biggest remuda, according to Luis Sanchez, would be under the tawny cliff northeast of the home place, and he was right. He should have been; no one including Jeff and Cal rode out as much as Luis did.

They saw the band about the same time the loose-stock saw riders approaching. From this point on the loose-stock would rely upon speed and the men would rely upon savvy. They could not run down a band of loose horses, slick as moles and as strong and durable as rawhide. Not atop horses which were carrying about two hundred and twenty pounds — except for Luis's mount. Sanchez did not weigh over a hundred and fifty or sixty pounds wringing wet, and he rode the best horse he could snake out to saddle up.

In fact it was Sanchez who left the others without a word, cutting straight eastward at a long lope. He was still holding that gait when the others could barely make him out, and the loose-stock was still a mile ahead.

The men swung off in scant tree shade to wait. A half hour later they saw the dust. A quarter hour after that they heard the ringing bare hooves striking like a symphony of iron against flinty land, and the loose-stock hove to view, travelling slower now, their first exuberance having been dissipated three miles eastward in the direction of the stageroad and the brakes.

Luis was nowhere in sight. He probably would not have been in any case, with all the dust at the drag.

Jeff and Lin Foster angled southward. Caloway Hamilton loped slowly northward, the direction the loose-stock would not take, but he went up there anyway, just in case, and also in order to be able to close with Luis when the horses raced past.

It was impossible to make an orderly drive

with horses full of early-morning spirit. The men had never attempted that. They waited until the first rush was over, then eased up, not to herd loose-stock, just to keep in sight of the leaders and gradually direct them in the correct direction. It was like a chess game, except that here, with eighty miles of open country, if the rangemen miscalculated, the loose-stock got a decent loophole, they would race away and it would take days to even find them again, let alone get them pointed correctly.

These men did not make mistakes. When the band sped past Lin and Jeff came in slightly, then dropped back as they made out Caloway bending the leaders, before the animals left him and he joined Luis in the drag.

It took two hours. Not just of riding; anyone could ride horses, all they had to do was spread their legs and yank a horse under them; it took two hours of move and counter-move, of playing chess, to manoeuvre the band to within sight of the buildings. By then the horses had been fairly well run out. Their leaders knew where they were going, had known it from the very beginning, but until now, glistening with sweat and sucking air, they had been unwilling.

Jeff raised a gloved hand as a signal. The

others dropped down to a little trot leaving the band to head on in by itself, uncrowded and finally resigned.

Two horses veered off but the others followed their leaders in past the wide gates and kept right on going all the way down the collection of corrals until they were milling and snorting in layers of dun dust in the farthest corral.

Luis veered off, out-manoeuvred the two loose horses and as the other men watched, he blocked them in every attempt to speed past, turned them, kept blocking each rush, and while Jeff and Cal laughed, Sanchez corralled the cut-backs, swung off, slammed the pole gate and turned without another glance to lead his mount to barn-shade for the unsaddling.

They had almost fifty head. Jeff and Cal made the division on foot, Cal on the gate, Jeff selecting and cutting-out into the adjoining corral. It was dusk when they finished, and two silent horsemen atop the northward cliff, up among tree-shadows where that flaked flint and obsidian from arrow-makers littered the forward ground, sat through the whole thing without a word, one of them grey and lined, chewing tobacco with slow rhythm, the other, a little younger, just beginning to show grey at the temples, smashed out his smoke atop the saddlehorn and dropped it, then peeled off gloves and lifted his hat to scratch as he said, "Well; they wasn't lyin'."

The older man spat before commenting. "I've heard of Rafter W stock before. Down in Colorado I once worked for an outfit had some Rafter W studs. Fine stock. Even from cold-blooded mares they got fine animals."

The taller man sighed and swung to the ground. He was wedge-shaped from raw-boned shoulders to lean hips. His attire was worn and faded, but his horse was breedy and built for speed. He would be worth a lot of money any place men wanted fast horses, which most stockmen did not want. They wanted short backs with lots of tough-ness and durability; speed was not very im-portant.

The older man also dismounted. He was thicker and more stooped; he was one of those deceptively slouching individuals, as tough as iron and without nerves anywhere in his carcass. He spat out the chewing tobacco and squinted a moment at the sun. "Sure would have helped if they hadn't taken that band. Did you follow that dust?"

The taller man had indeed followed the dust. "Right down to them buildings, Jas-per. Four fellers."

Jasper grunted. "Not just four fellers. That bunch knew exactly what they was doing, John. I'd rather steal horses from folks in town, or settlers, or even cowmen." For a moment the stooped older man studied the far buildings. "It ain't like stealin' chickens. Not in this kind of country. There's a town down yonder. You can see the sun bounce off glass winders and some of the rooftops. It's a hell of a long way from this horse outfit."

"What are you getting at?"

"We get caught back up in here, partner, and we're not going to no jailhouse. We're goin' to get hanged after dark, cut down and buried before sunrise. That's what I'm gettin' at."

John cast a look of mild annoyance at his partner. "You're talking like a scairy first-timer."

Jasper groped in a shirt pocket for his plug and bit off a fresh cud. After cheeking the tobacco he said, "That's why I'm as old as I am. Because I act like a scairy first-timer. And right now I'd say good as that band was, we'd better just lie over up here for a few days and pick out another bunch — and not go nowhere near that set of buildings."

They turned back off the cliff leading their horses almost two hundred yards to a creek-

26

bank where trout-minnows fled faster than lightning when four shadows loomed, two horses and two men, to bend and drink.

As they sat back, full and comfortable, Jasper said, "You ever see one of them old-time In'ians stuck up in a tree before?"

John shook his head to get rid of surplus creek water on his chin. "Nope."

"I was thinkin' back where we passed him — that old cuss must've been up there at least twenty years. A feller'd think winter snow and spring rain and all would have rotted that shrouding stuff they wrapped him in. . . . When I was a kid skinning buffler at three cents a head, we used to come onto them once in a while, only mostly they was put atop four poles in the ground."

John tossed aside his hat. It was wonderfully warm and pleasant there at the side of the grassy creek. "That's why you don't still find them; the poles rotted in the ground and the things fell down. Wolves would do the rest." He was not especially interested in the treed Indian. He was not, right at this moment, much interested in anything but lying there at peace, but he got up, hobbled his horse, dumped the saddle and bridle, then scooped water with his hat and washed the horse's back. The animal went right on eating despite the ice-water. He was about six or seven, judging from the curve of his chin and the lack of sunken places above his eyes. He was a handsome horse without a blemish showing anywhere.

Jasper also arose to care for his animal, but his movements were slower, more mechanical, as though he had done so much of this over the past forty-five years it had no longer any real significance to him. But it did have; no horsethief alive neglected caring for the one thing on this earth which could keep him alive — his four-legged piece of life insurance.

They went no farther from the cliff-face for a camp. There were no tracks anywhere up here, which meant the place was rarely visited. It was also possible for a man to walk over yonder and stand beside a big tree and watch the horses down below. Take his time about studying out exactly what had to be done.

If those riders had corralled that band of fifty or so head, then they were either going to be busy the next few days working them through corrals, or, better yet, they were going to make up a drive and head out with them. In the latter case, Jasper and John could make a leisurely sweep of Rafter W range, pick up the band they chose, and head westerly for about twenty miles before turning due southward down in the direction of Colorado.

With just a little luck they might never be pursued. It had happened before like this. But even if there was pursuit, it would be delayed.

Trackers would of course figure out what had happened. No horsethief expected not to be figured out. A man — or a pair of them — could not expect to drive away with a band of someone's loose-stock and not leave tracks behind them.

But seasoned horsethieves like John and his partner, knew the ways to use every advantage. Otherwise, as John had suggested, they would not still be at it.

But they were from Montana, did not know Long Grass Valley nor the best passes through the forty-mile-distant lower mountains. To John, there had to be a lot of time taken to make this raid work. He had always been a very deliberate and careful horsethief. Jasper was occasionally impatient, but after six years of partnering he was grudgingly coming round to John's way. There was one irrefutable piece of logic to this. They had never even come very close to being caught, and a man could not argue with success, especially when his life depended upon it.

They knew where they were going with the horses, in a very general way. Down through northern Colorado toward Denver where there was a big demand for good horses any time of the year, but they did not know the best, untravelled ways to get down there. What they really had to figure out was how to get across mostly treeless Long Grass Valley and through the southward mountains. After that, they could take a little more time.

3
PLANS

At fifty-five a man has everything he had in his youth, but with an added variety of wisdom, and depending upon the man, he was too wise or not wise enough. Being a horsethief at a time when they were hanged out of hand if caught on the open range, or sent to prison after being tried in towns, suggested that Jasper was maybe not wise enough. On the other hand he had been an outlaw for twenty years and had only been caught twice, once because he rode into a town where a wanted poster was nailed to the storefront only the day before, and the other time when he stole a band of prime redbacks. He got out of *that* scrape by accident; none of the Herefords was branded. Even the lawman who ran him down and brought him back was mad about that. Folks *knew* who those stolen cattle belonged to, but since most redbacks look alike and there was no mark to set this bunch apart, there had been no way to make the charge stick.

But Jasper White had never gone back there.

That time when he'd ridden in while his likeness on the poster was still fresh in everyone's mind, he had been taken with his back to the saloon door while relaxing with a drink. It had been the easiest imaginable capture. The deputy had simply walked up, shoved a gun in Jasper's back, lifted away Jasper's sixgun and marched him down to the jailhouse.

He'd had three hundred crisp greenbacks in his moneybelt. He and the deputy reached an agreement. That night Jasper escaped and rode fast — without his three hundred dollars.

That was another place he never returned to; but it was a vast country, between the Missouri River and Oregon, full of opportunities, like the one now facing Jasper down in Long Grass Valley, and as he sat with the taller and younger outlaw he was confident of success while he was also certain to be wary. He knew the price of being caught; had known other men who had paid that price at the end of a hardtwist rope.

As he'd said, horsethieves did not live long

unless they were as wary as lobo wolves.

John Hall could have given away nearly fifteen years to Jasper, but he still was greying around the temples and his face showed the same deep lines. He had been a rangerider for ten years, had suffered from it like they all did if they kept at it; a broken leg one time, and a cracked shoulder being bucked off in the rocks. He had cowboyed from Nogales to Burnt Timber in Montana and quit in disgust when he sat one night in a quiet poker game. He ran out of money. It was that simple. But in another way running out of money this particular night rankled because he'd had a very good hand without being able to play it. He'd gone to the bar to spend his last two-bits and over that one drink decided he was not getting younger, was never going to make any more than he was now making, and there had to be a better way for a man to use up his years.

He met Jasper White the following month in a sidehill camp near the Wyoming line. They had been riding together ever since, wraiths who rarely visited towns, who used game-trails rather than roadways, and left evidence of their shadowy passing in a number of empty corrals and thinned-down cattle herds.

It did in fact pay better. John spent a solid

one hundred dollars for that big bay horse, when good using stockhorses were going for anywhere between thirty and fifty dollars.

But lately he'd felt restless. As he told Jasper one night in camp, what the hell good was a pocketful of money if a man couldn't ride into a town of a Saturday night and let off steam?

Jasper had shrugged that off. He hadn't felt that way in a long while. "Someday," he replied, "you'll find just the right town, but it'll be a hell of a long way from where you ever been before. Just sit on the money until then."

John had gazed at his partner without saying a word, but if that were true, then how come old Jasper was still working, had never found that particular town, and he sure-Lord had ought to have by now.

Still, they had a good system; it had worked to perfection for a long time, and John's lack of wisdom was in the fact that he continued on out of strong habit, a professional outlaw because he had followed his trade until he forgot that he'd ever known any other trade.

As they loafed in camp the night after they had watched Rafter W bring in its horse-band, smoking and drinking coffee and drowsing before the little deadwood fire,

John said, "It'd be nice to own a horse ranch, Jasper. Live in a house and go to town when a man felt like it."

The older man did not dispute that. Once, years back, he'd felt the same way. He'd never done anything about it but occasionally, when he'd see some cowman or horseman driving to town with his woman and their pups in the wagon, the thought came briefly to life again.

"Takes a lot of money to set up," was about all he said this particular night. In the back of his mind there was another drawback; when a man is accustomed to having several hundred dollars in his pockets, stepping down to hoeing beans and wearing patched britches and working hard from before dawn until after sundown, unable to get free of debt, then a family and hardship did not seem so good. Did not in fact seem like a good life at all.

But he knew the symptoms in his younger partner, and all the talk in the world would not get that idea out of John's head. Only time could do that. Jasper was wise in this too.

But no man is wise about all things. As they sat propped in the starbright night Jasper said, "We got it down to where it works every time. Why spoil it? We're goin' to make a real killing one of these times; have money comin' out our ears."

John yawned, let this subject pass, and twisted to see where the horses had got to. They were still within the reflection of the flames. He drained the last of the liquid and flung the dregs aside, then pulled grass to cleanse the tin cup before turning it face-down upon a stone near the fire as he said, "Those horses had ought to make a killing. Is that what you meant?"

Jasper shook his head slowly, the way a man would do who is keeping something to himself, had in fact been keeping something to himself for a long while.

"Not off the horses," he murmured. "Not off any horse-band. Not even off cattle. A real killing; more money'n you can carry."

John detected the change of tone and looked around. He also saw the changed expression in the red-gold firelight. "What you up to?" he asked, because when two men had ridden side by side as long as these two had they got to know one another's idiosyncrasies very well.

Jasper raised pale grey unwavering eyes without lifting his head. "A bank."

For a moment longer they stared at one another. Finally John made a nervous giggle. "How long you been figurin' on this,

Jasper?" The idea had shocked him. "You mean — a bank in a town?"

Jasper ignored the sudden signs of wide-awake astonishment. "You'd work a tenth as hard as stealin' livestock. You'd work maybe a half hour, then you'd ride out and run for it without no damned horses nor cattle to hold you back. And you could carry all the money you'd need for the rest of your life inside your shirt."

John had been drowsy, a little bored with their earlier conversation but he was wide awake now. "What bank?" he asked, fishing for the makings to roll a smoke.

Jasper had no particular bank in mind so he said, "It don't make a lot of difference. Find one, study it out like we do with the horses and cattle. Be careful and take plenty of time. Then raid it. . . . but in the late afternoon, you see, so's we'll be riding through the night. No one can catch us in the darkness and come morning they'll have tracks, but for eight or ten hours we'll be widening the lead. . . . Then, shuck the horses, take a train and go all the way back to Dodge City, or maybe to Chicago. Anywhere. We'll have money enough to go anywhere." Jasper thinly smiled. "You want a horse ranch — you can just walk up and lay down the greenbacks for it."

John smoked and gazed out into the yonder night, then lifted his range a little to include the far rims and the rosary of stars draped up there. Finally he said, "I never thought of a bank, Jasper."

"Forget it," the older outlaw said, perfectly convinced John could not forget it. "It'd be dangerous."

"What ain't?" shot back lanky John Hall, and spat into the fire, listened to the sizzle then smiled across at Jasper. "You're sly, Jas. You're a sly old bastard. How long you been thinking on this?"

"Oh, since last winter when we was running out of money and there was three-foot snowbanks everywhere a man looked. . . . I got to figurin' that while we're doin' well — a damned sight better'n any butt-froze rangerider ever did — we're not gettin' younger and what we need is one hell of a big one. Big enough so's afterwards we won't never have to look at snow or camp under trees again as long as we live. . . . For a tenth the work we'll come out with fifty times as much money."

"Or get shot."

Jasper brushed that aside. "Hell; a man can get shot any Saturday night in a saloon — or get hanged stealin' horses, which is worse. Thing is, John — the risk would not be one darned bit more. It would be *less* to my way of figurin' things."

John pitched the cigarette stub into the dying little cooking-fire. "What bank? Don't tell me you didn't have some bank in mind."

"They got one in that town we seen from the cliff. The town's name is Cutler. They got a sort of bank down there."

John gazed steadily. "I thought you said you'd never been down through here before."

"I ain't. But a feller I rode with before you and me teamed up, he came from around here somewhere. He was the one told me they had a sort of bank down at Cutler. Told me a lot about the town too."

"What's a — sort-of bank?"

"It ain't a real one; it don't have no brass grilles and all, but it's in the back of the general store run by the same feller who looks after the mail. They been storin' up money for townsmen and stockmen in there for a long time. Years."

John began a slow smile. "Jasper, tell me something: When we come down here, did you figure to steal horses, or raid this bank?"

Jasper grinned crookedly. "I figured we'd do one or the other, but I was goin' to leave it up to you. I can't do it alone. One feller's got to be inside stuffin' money in a sack and one feller's got to be outside with the horses and keepin' an eye on folks . . . they got a town marshal down there, but he won't make us no trouble."

"Why won't he?"

"I already told you — we raid the bank at suppertime. No noise, no shooting, just walk in and throw down and maybe knock someone over the head, or leave 'em tied and gagged. No one'll know what's goin' on. Won't be customers in the store just short of closing time. We likely won't even see that town marshal."

John laughed and shook his head at his partner. "All right, Jasper."

The older man fished forth his cut plug to whittle off a sliver and shove it into his cheek. Then he said, "We got to get new horses. That's where those animals down below fit in."

John protested. "Not a thing wrong with my bay. Sound as new money, strong as a bear and fast as hell."

Jasper gently wagged his head. "John, that horse has been slowin' down the last year. He's had a lot of hard riding lately. So has my horse. We're riskin' the whole darned shooting-match on this one pitch of the dice, and we're not going to take one single damned chance we don't have to take. . . .

Tomorrow we'll go down and skirt in and out among them foothills and look over the loose-stock. Rafter W's got some mighty fine animals. We're not going to take no risks we don't have to take."

But John did not relent easily. "I paid a hunnert damned dollars for that horse, Jasper."

"I know that. Listen to me; this is the biggest toss of the dice we're ever going to make. Just one pitch for the rest of our lives. We're not goin' into it on the best horses in the world if they are wore down and a little tired. We just can't do it like that. This time, by gawd, we got to make better than we ever did before, and not take one single chance."

John sat in thoughtful silence for a long while. He would agree, and Jasper knew he would, but the whole idea was still new. It would take anyone a spell to get used to the notion. With John, when he finally got completely involved, he would agree to avoid all risks.

Jasper peered into his tin cup. There were a couple of swallows left. He up-ended the tin cup, swallowed acidy black coffee and tossed the cup down without bothering to clean it as his partner had done. It had been a long day and he was tired.

4
HORSES AND MEN

There were places, in parts of Mexico but not north of there, where a tiny ribbon was braided into the mane of horses directly behind the ear. The colour of the ribbon denoted whether a horse was broke to ride, was green as grass, or was being reined.

It would have helped when Jasper and John slipped down into the brakes below the tawny cliff and slowly passed along until they located a couple of bands of Rafter W horses. But neither of the outlaws had ever seen any of those little coloured ribbons nor had even heard of the practice of braiding them into manes.

They judged whether a horse was saddle-broke or not by other methods. Commonly by the little white patches of hair around the withers, denoting much use — and usually the result of carelessness and negligence because those white hairs grew out of old saddle-sores.

There were other ways to tell, but a logical rule-of-thumb on a horse ranch was to assume any horse four or better was broke. Cowmen might let un-used horse-flesh eat up their grass because they hadn't got round to breaking them, but horsemen didn't. They only kept riding or working or combination horses they could handle and use and peddle. Spoiled or unbroke four or five-year-olds, were either blemished and unsound or not worth breaking, and usually they were peddled to wolfers or some other hunters who baited traps or lures with red meat.

Still, as Jasper said while he and John Hall were belly-down in pale, tall buffalo-grass atop a low knoll, watching a band south of them a quarter mile, it would be best if they could steal a top horse out from under someone; then they could be absolutely certain they were getting exactly what they needed.

John kept studying the placid band of sleek animals. "We can find out anyway, once we pick them out and rope 'em. Ain't a horse alive a man can't ride for one full day and not know if he's got bad habits or not."

That was true, providing the man did not ride the horse in a small, inhibiting corral.

Jasper pulled off his hat and let it drop in the grass while he raised up, lizard-like to squint against the bright sunlight down yonder. For a long while he simply looked, then he eased back and said, "Good stock, John. By golly that's good stock out there."

John, a more practical person, studied the band, picked through it without opening his mouth, and finally said, "Let's mosey on around. It's prime stock all right but we only seen this one band so far. Let's go see what else they got down here."

They were in no hurry, and this idea appealed to Jasper who was careful when he had to be, and all other times was prudent.

He hadn't slept for a while last night but had looked up at the endless heavens turning a lot of details over in his mind. *This* was what he had decided long ago he had to do; make one big raid. His last big raid. Get enough money to never have to sleep on the ground again if he did not want to.

Age, he knew from having more of it than a lot of folks had, was really more a condition of mind than of body, providing a man never softened and in Jasper's trade there was rarely either the time or the opportunity to sit all winter somewhere eating and drinking, playing poker and courting dance-hall girls.

He was sinewy and strong; as durable as an old piece of green hide. That slouched stoop was a deception which he had developed over the years. But — after enough years, a man expected more from life than just forever working at his trade. He wanted to sit on hotel porches smoking two-bit cigars wearing a nice broad-cloth coat and hand-made calfskin boots with a ring on his finger and an engraved gold pocket-watch, and across his belly a fine gold chain to go with it.

And sleep indoors. And eat in hotel dining-rooms. It wasn't age, it was just something a man finally decided he had earned.

As for the bands of horses they rode around and scouted up, that was part of it. This time, when he rode in, he would be riding the best horse he could find. That would, in fact, be his opening card in the new game he was now going to play.

Risk? Hell's bells he had never in his life existed in an environment where risk and peril were not more than arms' distance away.

When they were sitting saddles in a bosque of second-growth pines about five miles west around the high curve of the valley watching the fourth band of horses they had scouted-up since early morning, he said, "The horses will be the easiest part of it, John. Them fellers who took in that band yesterday will be busy as a kitten in a box of shavings for a few days. Even if they don't trail them out. We don't even have to make our choice today. We got plenty of time to make this come off perfect."

John lit a cigarette still eyeing the unsuspecting herd south of the tree-fringe. "Go on," he said.

"We can ride down to the town and see how things look."

John trickled smoke and nodded his head, still looking out yonder. Having come in on this idea of Jasper's he was ready, as usual, to leave the initiative to the older man. "Tomorrow," he said, and finally looked elsewhere, out across the miles of open countryside. There was not a rider nor a building in sight as far as a man could see. Just grass and sunshine and little bunches of horses, and the uplands at the back of all of it. A clean, unspoilt country.

They started back, keeping to the trees, and in among the broken country all the way. A solitary rider appeared, once, out where that first band had been. John thought it was a young boy but Jasper shook his head. He had seen this same slight figure before, yesterday between the loose-stock and the cliff-face, riding in the drag of those driven animals.

"It's a man," he said, watching that distant horseman. "Small, but it's a man all right."

They remained stationary to avoid detection even though they were in moving sky-shadows among the brakes near stands of spindly trees.

The loose-stock saw that solitary horseman, but did not race away because he sensed the exact moment they were verging upon flight, and halted out there to sit gazing at them. Jasper said, "No kid's got that much experience," referring to the way that rangerider had known precisely when he could not go another step closer.

The rider sat a while, then turned and rode westerly. "Makin' a sashay," muttered Jasper, whose interest in the distant rider was acute. "I thought yesterday they was pretty savvy, them fellers." He sounded more cautious than usual. "Didn't figure anyone would ride out today, after they took in that band yesterday. Figured they'd be busy at the corrals."

When the rider was fading, they turned on up the trail without additional conversation until they were back beyond the bluff at their creek-side camp, then as Jasper off-saddled he looked thoughtful.

"Maybe it's just that one feller who rides out every day or so and tallies them horses. There's always one busybody in every riding crew."

John's concern had been shaped by his partner's interest. "We could go somewhere else to get new horses," he said, "but I sure seen some down there I'd give a lot to straddle."

Jasper shook his head. "We won't find any others as good."

"Then we'd better make damned certain that feller don't ride up and maybe find he's short a couple of animals when we're ready to ride."

Jasper dumped his saddle horn-down and cantle up as he said, "We got the time. We'll study it out." That was his way of being reassuring, not only to his partner but to himself.

They loafed away what was left of the afternoon, cared for their animals then made an early supper and went on foot back to the edge of the cliff to look downward, out and around on all sides.

Dusk was coming but there was still a glow of late-day sunshine, only now it lacked the brilliance and therefore also lacked the eye-squinting reflections. They could barely make out Cutler off to the southeast. It was while they were slouching there among the trees that Jasper said, "We got to light out early, before sunup, so's to be across Rafter W to the stageroad before folks are stirring. No one's going to wonder about a couple of fellers travelling down the road like all folks travel, but if someone from Rafter W was to see us angling across their range, they'd wonder . . . They aren't goin' to know there was anyone up here at all, until we're long gone."

John yawned and watched those distant ranch buildings. "That's the kind of place I'd like to have someday. Good log buildings and plenty of corrals, and shade trees round the yard."

Jasper turned his attention to Jeff Wayman's home-place and half-smiled. "When you're ready, you'll just ride in and peel the greenbacks out of your moneybelt and buy 'em out."

John sighed. "You sure we're goin' to get that much out of Cutler?"

"We'll find out tomorrow, or the next day; we'll hang around down there until we *do* find out. If they don't have that much down there, we'll find a town an' a bank, that does have. This time, by gawd, we're not goin' to eat dust behind some lousy horses or lumbering, stupid redbacks."

They ambled back, John beginning to savour the feel of all the money he could carry, beginning to think in terms of his horse ranch, and some other things he planned to go with it but which he would not mention to Jasper again — a woman and maybe a new saddle with silver on it, respect in the towns and flashy boots and hats and even one of those Prince Albert frock coats gamblers and undertakers wore. And a ring for his left hand of solid gold. And only pure black horses, his favourite colour in animal-flesh.

He bypassed the leggy big bay with scarcely a glance. Normally he was solicitous of this animal, not because it was a good one, especially, although that certainly had always been important to him, but because he had paid more for the bay than he had ever before paid for *two* horses in his life.

Jasper, who took care of mounts because he knew they were essential and had to be in good condition every moment, was satisfied to see the animals peacefully grazing inside their rawhide hobbles. He dropped down where they had made their cooking-fire stone-ring and stirred ash without finding any coals, and went to work whittling shavings.

It had been a magnificent early-summer day and seemed likely to be a pleasant evening and maybe even a warm night, although that might be expecting more than folks had a right to expect this early in the summer.

When Jasper had the little smokeless fire going he rummaged saddlebags for coffee and tinned peaches, some little baled dried apples that looked as dark as his plug of chewing tobacco, and dipped water from the creek to boil the apples in. They only had three cooking utensils, the little pan, a small skillet and their dented old coffeepot, just large enough for two cups at a time.

When John returned from a walk farther back, over beyond the creek and out through a stand of spindly wood where he could see the high country, through which they had made their way a few days back, he dropped down to watch his partner and to work up a smoke which he lit with a curling firebrand from the stone-ring.

"It's like the first time I ever went on a raid," he told Jasper, speaking casually of a confidential sensation. The more he thought of the rewards of this one raid, the more excited he became over the prospects of actual wealth. "Why the hell didn't we figure on this before?"

Jasper poked the swelling apples with a stick. They still did not look very appetising but the aroma was pleasant. He put the stick aside to use a boot-knife in ripping away the lid of the peach-tin. "Takes time to get where we are now," he replied, sawing at the stubborn tin. "Why don't they dry these damned peaches like they do the apples?" The lid came free and Jasper ruefully looked at the cutting edge of his bootknife. "Now it won't cut hot butter," he mumbled, returning the knife to its scabbard and offering John the peach tin. "We been gettin' along pretty well. Thing is, a man gets up as high in a trade as he can get and once he's there he's either got to stay right there and never do no better, or he's got to figure out something new. Like a bank. Or maybe a bullion stage. Only them stages usually got gunguards all over them, inside and atop too. Banks is right in towns. Folks walk in and out all day long." He took back the peach tin, drank the last of the syrup and mouthed halves of peaches.

The apples were boiling so he set them aside before they fell apart and used the same stick to stir frying meat in their small skillet.

"They could have guards down there at that bank," said John.

Jasper doubted it. "Naw; but that's what we're going down to find out. And where the lawman spends his late afternoons and evenings. Hell; the James boys and the Daltons — dozens of fellers made it rich off banks."

It was not the best of all comparisons, after what had happened up at Northfield in Minnesota when the James gang was nearly wiped out, a recollection still fresh in people's minds. Jasper realised the moment after speaking he had said the wrong thing, so he pushed right on to also say, "We aren't going in in broad daylight, either. We're going to figure this right down to the least detail. We're going to come out it without a scratch and with money to burn." He put the tin pan of boiled apples between them and hauled the fry-pan off the fire too, which left only the blackened little dented coffeepot. As they ate, using fingers and their knives, John seemed care-free. He was no doubt embarking again on a flight of fancy. The idea had been surprising and daring last night. This morning it had been pleasant, and by this evening it was a glow which kept his mind and heart pleasantly warm.

"What you goin' to do?" he asked, and got a dry glance from the older outlaw.

"Nothin', not even any plannin', until I got the money in my hands and two, three hunnert miles between me'n that town down there."

"All right. But after that what are you going to do, Jasper? You're not goin' in on this just because you want to hold a sack full of greenbacks in your hands."

"No," conceded the older man, and chewed a moment before speaking again. "I'm going to buy some elegant clothes, a pair of nice black calfskin boots, a pocketful of two-bit stogies, then take the train-cars maybe back as far as Chicago and find me a barbershop like they got in Fort Worth where when they finish shaving and shearin' you they sprinkle lavender water on you." He stopped, gazed across the settling dusk at his partner, and smiled widely, something he rarely did. "Then maybe I'll just set and rattle, and tell folks I'm a banker and watch how they treat me."

John laughed. The story had no real goal; not the way his dream had, and what tickled him most was a vision of Jasper wearing a fine suit and smelling of that lavender water. "You'll find a woman too," he said. "When a man's got that kind of money, he can't stay free of them."

Jasper shrugged. "We'll see," was all he'd

commit himself to. "I was married once."

John's smile died. "You never told me that."

"Why should I? Anyway, it was a long time back and she died. We was married two years. We was crossing over down at Council Bluffs with a wagonload of our gatherings. . . . She got the lung fever down there in the mud-flats. There was a hell of a lot of it going around that spring. Folks was dyin' off like flies. . . . Well; I buried her on the far side and kept on drivin' for a month, then just — let it all go. Lost most of it in a poker session at Bridger's place, bought two horses, packed one, rode the other one, and come on after that." Jasper finished eating and restlessly shifted position. "I wish to hell we had some whisky. That's another bad thing about livin' out of your saddle-bags; you never got enough room for more'n a pony at a time and I drink that much at one lousy setting."

John understood better than Jasper would have thought. "We'll get a damned gallon of the stuff when we're safe out of the damned country with our bank money, Jas. . . . The night we set down and have a big supper somewhere we'll buy us a gallon of the best whisky they make . . . Then we'll split up, eh?"

Jasper kept gazing into the fire as he nodded his head without saying another word.

5
CUTLER

Cutler had two brick storefronts. One at the hotel, which was an old log barracks on three sides with bricks in front facing the roadway. The other brick front was on the jailhouse, and it too had log walls on the remaining three sides.

There were half-grown shade trees, the product of an old man's foresight back quite a few years, because otherwise there were no trees out that far across Long Grass Valley.

The town had been growing since it had been a freight way-station and army camp a generation back. It had never been a fort, as many other frontier towns had been. But it had housed three troops of horse-soldiers and one mountain howitzer company among its spaced log hutments and buildings. The town had grown from these structures. Now, the old log buildings were in the centre of Cutler, but back some years they had been at both ends of the settlement.

It should have been named after some general or maybe some territorial bigwig. Instead, it had got its name from a man no one knew and even the scant handful of oldtimers still hobbling around who had seen him, had not known his name.

He had been a hide-hunter and dealer. By trade he was a man who made skinning knives out of horseshoe rasps and anything else which was fitting and available. Folks had called the place 'the cutler's camp' back then. Since those days they had simply abandoned the two words 'the' and 'camp'. The village and eventually the town became known as Cutler. There was no way to make anything very momentous or heroic out of that, but a few generations hence folks would try. It wasn't very exalting living in a place founded by a dirty, smelly old knife-sharpener who scratched, shooed flies, and sharpened knives when he wasn't disembowelling and skinning stiff buffalo corpses.

Craig Stanton knew all the oldtimers who were still around, which was precious few and they got fewer with each coming spring-time. He had become over the recent years local historian-of-note. He did not mind; in fact he had a leaning towards local history,

58

probably because as township marshal he had blessed little to do from autumn until springtime, and in the summertime even though there were dozens more rangemen arriving in town Saturday nights, Craig Stanton at two hundred and ten pounds and six feet and two inches, normally had to do no more than appear in a doorway without smiling.

He was down at the harness shop in the late afternoon killing time with the saddle-maker, watching with idle interest the day-long quiet roadway get progressively more quiet as suppertime approached. The only men out there were a pair of strangers, rangemen from their soiled, faded appearance, one taller and probably younger astride a handsome big bay horse, the other older, greyer and lined, stooped at the shoulders, riding a seal-brown gelding leaned down like a wolf from hard use.

The pair of them poked southward in no hurry. Itinerant riders were like autumn leaves, they drifted in, drifted on again, cut from the east or west, mostly from the warmer southern territories, and they looked pretty much the same.

As Marshal Stanton said to the saddler, "Those two must have wintered in Montana to be arrivin' from the north."

The saddler did not even glance up. "Drifters; always ridin' into a new place, and in the autumn ridin' out again. What do they expect to amount to? Nothin' more shiftless than saddlebums."

Craig Stanton watched the pair of strangers out of sight. "Men do what they know. If ridin' is all, why then they keep right on doing it."

The saddle-maker finally raised tough old dark eyes while he made a contradiction. "Naw. We all done that one time or another. Some of us got sense after a while and learnt a trade. You can ride until you're so old the ranches find a hunnert excuses for not hirin' you on, and you'll never have enough money to do anything but get drunk Saturday night." The saddler pointed. "See them saddles and headstalls? Every darned one's been left here by some rangerider who busted them, got me to repair 'em, then just never came back. I got an old A-fork Texas outfit in the backroom I had since I first opened up. You know how long ago that was, Craig? Thirty-one years last January."

The lawman considered. "He's dead by now, whoever he was."

The saddle-maker scraped stiffening beeswax from thick, stained fingers. "And if I give that old outfit to some kid, you know what'd happen?"

Craig smiled. "He'd walk in tomorrow and demand his saddle."

"You are dead right. I figured it up one time; I got better'n sixty dollars tied up in them unclaimed outfits."

"You could hold a sheriff's sale."

The saddle-maker sniffed. "But I won't."

That ended the discussion which had begun when Jasper White and John Hall had slouched into town in the cooling late afternoon.

Craig Stanton ambled back to the roadway. There was no sign of the strangers, but they would no doubt be putting up their stock down at the liverybarn. It did not mean anything to him one way or the other. He went over to the general store and leaned on the counter while the proprietor counted up his money and stuffed it into a little soiled flour sack. The storekeeper said, "You'd figure folks from out over the range would be flockin' in now that the ridin' season's in full swing with new crews to be fed and all." He shook his head. "Business has been as slow as molasses in January so far this spring." He turned to take the floursack back where an old man with black cotton sleeve protectors was drowsing at a small counter. Behind the old man was a large, massive steel safe painted dull grey and with a very improbable blood-red sunset in oil paint across its mighty steel door. "Chuck it in," the storekeeper said, pitching his soiled flour sack atop the counter.

Craig bought a sack of tobacco and leaned while he built a cigarette. "Anyone sold stock yet?" he asked in a tone of near-indifference.

The storekeeper shook his head, then his dolorous long face briefly brightened. "Too early for the big drives, but young Wayman has contracted thirty head of sound geldings, so when he gets paid he'll be along to put in the money. That'll be a start."

Marshal Stanton blew smoke. "He's not the only one'll have his money in there."

"Oh no," agreed the storekeeper. "There's money left over from the drive last autumn." His little happy looked returned, but as before only briefly. "I make better bankin' fees every year. It's been growin' right well the past fifteen, eighteen years. I been thinking, maybe I'll sell the store someday and just go to banking."

Marshal Stanton gazed through slow-rising grey smoke, his expression sceptical. "You'll starve, Caleb. Maybe someday, but I doubt like hell you could live off bankin' charges now."

"I didn't say I was going to sell out the store tomorrow. It's just something I carry in the back of my head. Maybe for when I am old as Frank, back there with his darned cotton sleeve-protectors. Too old to want to move around much. And Cutler will grow, you can mark my word for it. We'll get a telegraph line in here one of these days, and maybe, while you and I are still around, a set of railroad tracks. More cattle too, and more horse-outfits. Cutler's set just right to handle growth, Craig."

Marshal Stanton had been listening to this kind of talk ever since arriving to hire on as local law officer, and while he had seen some growth-changes anyway — there was still nothing more than talk about a tele-graph station ever reaching Cutler. As for that railroad line . . . He straightened up off the counter . . . "I'm not sure we really need those things, Caleb."

"Sure we do. That's progress."

Craig did not argue. He was not inclined by nature to be argumentative. After stroll-ing out into the quiet early evening he tried to guess what the difference was between 'progress' and just plain 'growth', shrugged it off and headed across the road to his jail-house office where he had left the stove smouldering all day and was now glad he had because it seemed that the night was not going to be as pleasant and balmy as the previous couple of nights had been.

He chucked in a half-log of dead oak and positioned his coffeepot atop the stove, then went over to sink his smoke in the watery spittoon behind his desk and sat down, flung his hat aside and regarded the unkempt condition of the desk-top.

He hated writing letters above every other thing connected with his job. He had completed very little school and could not spell worth a dang. He also had no particular filing system, but as long as he could get empty crates from Caleb over at the store he made out by stuffing everything which came in the mail into crates. Wanted dodgers in one set of boxes, letters of enquiry he would answer some day, into other boxes, random mailings into another set of crates. He now had three big dry-goods crates full of wanted posters and he had yet to hunt down a single one of those fugitives. Mainly because he had not seen any of those men, that he knew of anyway, around Cutler, but also because hunting down men just to be manhunting had never appealed to him very much. Not even when they had bounties on their scalps.

There was no reason for a man to work himself into an early grave. He'd get there soon enough, and meanwhile he could enjoy stoves in winter and sunshine in summertime, jokes and drinks with rangemen now and then, and gossip the rest of the time around Cutler.

The storekeeper considered him lazy. He knew it. In fact the cranky blacksmith at the eastern side of town on down the wide roadway, had once told him to his face he thought lawmen went into that kind of work because they didn't want to use a muscle they did not have to use.

Big Craig Stanton had smiled indulgently downward. The cranky blacksmith was built like an oaken barrel but he was easily a foot shorter and fifteen years older. Anyway, Craig, who was honest with himself, thought he was probably right, and it did not bother Craig at all.

But the letters on the desk had to be attended to *sometime.* This was the middle of the week; the beginning of the riding season without another blessed thing for him to do, so he hitched up his mighty shoulders, reached for the pencil stub and went to work.

Amid the letters were four wanted posters from Montana. They had either reproduced photographs on them or drawings. One of them made Craig sit and stare and rack his brains. He thought he might have seen this man somewhere. *Thought* he had, but hell, if it were true it could have been a year back. The fugitive was certainly not around Cutler now.

He was wanted for horsetheft, rustling cattle, for two shootings, one fatal, and looked out at Craig from a pair of dead-calm pale eyes, a face held forward as though the outlaw were stooped at the shoulders, and there was a three hundred dollar bounty on him. Among the other things he had done it said he had escaped from jail one time. Another time he had been tried and acquitted for rustling.

His name was given as Jasper White.

Craig yawned, swung around and plunged all four of those dodgers into one of the crates reserved for these posters, then he swung back and took up the pencil again. There was no longer any way to avoid writing the letters.

It took almost two full hours and he grudged every moment of it. Once, he'd tried to charm the school-ma'm into at least helping him with this work. She had turned him down with a flat "No! And you ought to be ashamed of yourself, a grown man and all, not being able to compose letters and spell words!"

Well; she was as homely as a mud wall anyway.

6
A New Season

Caleb Hotchkiss's father had started the general store in Cutler. He had in fact been the freighter who had bought hides from the old cutler from whom the town had been indirectly named. He had been a taciturn man who spoke neither of his past nor of the men he had associated with back in those early days, so while Caleb might have known a lot of early-day anecdotes, he in fact knew none, and it did not bother him at all.

He had taken over the store at his father's death, had brought it out of the trading-post category by bringing in bolt goods and the first bleached flour anyone in Long Grass Valley had ever seen, and he had prospered from the first year.

He had never married — unless it had been his store — and had over the years come to resemble his father more and more, without being aware of it. He was humourless, smiled mechanically, and extended almost no credit nor took more than a simulated interest in the community. He liked handling money, making a profit, working with figures which represented hard cash.

He was not the most admired man in Cutler but people traded with him because they had no second choice. He knew that too, and it pleased him to hold that kind of power.

He had been a trademan all his life and could tell at first glance how much he could charge, so when the stooped, unshaven grizzled rangerider with the faded clothes and dead-calm grey eyes sidled to his counter to purchase two plugs of chewing tobacco, Cal tossed them down, quoted the price and waited.

The grey-headed cowboy represented the same thing to Cal Hotchkiss he would have represented to the harness-maker. One of those saddle-tramps who came and went like autumn leaves until they got too old to be hired on. Cal privately held rangemen in contempt, but in a country dominated by them he rarely let it show. Now, as the cowboy dropped a small coin Cal scooped it into his cash drawer and turned away.

The grizzled rangeman watched his

progress, read him exactly right, then let his gaze drift back where old Frank was dozing on his stool in front of the big iron safe, his black cotton sleeve protectors a precursor of the black armbands his few friends would wear shortly now at Frank's passing.

The location of the safe was favourable; in the back of the big old barn of a store where shadows hung throughout the brightest day, far enough from the doorway and the roadside windows to be out of sight after sundown.

Its size was impressive. Jasper loafed as he gnawed a corner off one of his plugs and cheeked it while slowly pocketing the plug. A safe that large in a thrifty cattle-range area had to hold considerable wealth. He turned and slouched back out into the sun-bright morning, stooped and unkempt and calm in his slow, thoughtful appraisal of the town.

Then he ambled off in the direction of the cafe where John was already eating. But they sat at opposite ends of the counter and completely ignored each other.

Craig Stanton finished breakfast before either of those cowboys did, paid up and strolled over across the road in the direction of the stage company's office. All the outside news arrived over there first, either in the form of a newspaper now and then, or gossip. The man who ran the office and adjoining yard was one of those individuals who seemed to attract information without seeming to make an effort in this regard.

When he saw big Craig Stanton coming he removed his pipe, spat into the dust of the yard and walked down as far as the front gate to say, "Morning. Beautiful day."

Craig agreed, but with a reservation. "We could use some rain the next week or so."

The older, shorter man was indifferent about that, for while he recognised the need for water to keep the grass coming, rainfall also upset his schedules and made the roads greasy and cloying, things someone at this trade could not be expected to like.

"Did you know young Jeff Wayman's sold some geldings to a buyer who's staying over at the rooming-house?"

Craig smiled. For once he had the gossip before his friend had it. "Yeah, I heard that. Who's the buyer — you know him?"

"Feller named Hastings from over around Fort Sheridan, that's all I know. Except that he hired a couple of the riders hangin' around town to take the herd out for him. It's a good start for the season, though, wouldn't you say?"

Craig turned wary. "If everyone else sells

too, and the prices stay up. Not just for horses but for cattle too . . . Got to be rain though, and no more frost at night."

"It's gettin' late in the season for freezin' nights," replied the stage-company's Cutler manager. "Look at that sunshine. Warms things a foot down." He smiled slightly. "A man gets tired of winter, and after August he gets tired of summer. I grew up in south Texas; we had so damned much summer a man never quit sweatin' and when I pulled out I promised myself I'd find a place with four seasons."

Craig was not that fond of winter but he simply said, "I guess you got to have the seasons to make it possible to keep things living." He glanced beyond, out in the centre of the yard where two soiled hostlers had a coach on jacks with all four wheels off. "What happened?" he asked, and the shorter man turned.

"Damned soft axles," he exclaimed, his tone changing. "There was a time when blacksmiths took pride in their work. Not no more. Who ever heard of two axles going soft at the same time, under the same coach. And that's a hell of a job, pullin' them and fitting in another pair. And for all I know the next pair'll be ten per cent lead too." He made a little fluttery gesture of despair with his hands. "I should have never let the company supply me. I should have had axles made right here in town where the smith's still got his pride and all."

"Otherwise how is business?" the lawman asked, still watching those two swearing men back there working at removing axle-housings and hangers.

The older man thought over his answer before offering it. "The passenger end is lousy, but then it's never been good here. We're too far from the cities and railroads. Only peddlers, a few rangemen, buyers sometimes, and folks going on through, ride the coaches. But the light freight business is pretty fair. Except in wintertime. We hauled in six crates for Hotchkiss so far this week, and that'll pay the wages and keep feed in the mangers." He looked up. "How's the law business — quiet as usual?"

Craig's eyes dropped to the older man's face. This was not the only businessman in town who grudgingly paid his share of the town's administrative expenses. They all thought the same — if there had been any safe way to eliminate the town marshal's job they would vote to do it. But if they did, and trouble came. . . .

"Routine," he said, and smiled directly into the older man's eyes. "Until the day arrives when someone robs one of your stages."

After this he continued his round of Cutler, halting for a cup of coffee with the harness-maker who always seemed less dour in the early morning. He'd been reading in an old newspaper about two men stealing cattle and horses up in Montana last summer and being so successful at it that the Montana authorities had hired the Pinkerton Detective Agency over in St Louis to catch the rustlers.

"And by gawd not even the Pinkertons could find them. Now you know, those boys got to be smart as hell. The Pinkertons don't fail too often."

Craig sipped his coffee. "As long as they keep it up in Montana," he said, and put the cup down, not very interested. "You starting a new saddle?"

The harness-maker put his newspaper aside and gazed at the pale, new leather he'd left under small sandbags overnight. "Trying something new, Craig. I'm going to finish all the rigging *beneath* the swell-covering and skirts this time." He strolled to the workhouse with its bindings and racheted lever on the right side. "For years I been wondering if there warn't some way to protect the rigging-leathers. Darned rangeman never take care of anything; dump their saddles in the dirt, leave 'em out in the rain and snow — then come in here cussin' because the rigging leather got rotten and when some horse crow-hopped with them, the leather busted." He lifted the swell-covering a little to show the straps beneath, which normally would have been put across the top of the fork on the outside.

Craig was intrigued by the idea. "By golly, I think you've come up with something at that. I never saw a saddle with the rigging underneath before."

The harness-maker smiled. "Neither have I. But the idea's been in the back of my mind for a long while." He ran a rough, scarred and stained big hand over the leather, gently.

"Who you making it for?"

"No one, just makin' it is all, Craig. Hell, if I done this to some saddle I'd been hired to make I'd catch hell. Folks fight change." The grin lingered. "I do too, but at least in this thing I know what I'm doing and why it had ought to be done." He looked around. "You need a new saddle by any chance?"

Craig laughed and shook his head. The harness-maker nodded at him. "That's it, you see. I know that old saddle of yours, and maybe you like this idea and maybe you're just bein' polite, but anyway — you don't want to take a chance. Well; maybe I'll end up keepin' it for myself."

Craig said, "You don't ride out. I haven't seen you on a horse in five, six years."

"Then I'll hang it up. Someday a greenhorn will walk in and I'll peddle it to him."

The morning was advancing. One of those faded-looking rangemen Craig had seen at the cafe was over in front of the gunsmith's shop, leaning against an overhang upright, smoking. He was tall and did not look more than thirty-five. He did not look especially hard-pressed; at least the way he was leaning indolently gave that impression.

The morning coach cut southward from the corral-yard down the road, two men on the high-seat, and the leather flap over the rear boot rolled up and tied in place, indicating there was no light freight leaving town.

The sun climbed steadily, warmth spilled outward and downward from it in all directions and the air was so clear Marshal Stanton could see all the way over to those brindle bluffs behind the Wayman place.

In another month or two there would be hazy afternoons caused by rising heat. Summer would be across the land in all its strength.

Rigging *beneath* the fork coverings and rear skirts. . . . He shook his head and ambled over across the wide roadway heading for his office. He had to sweep the place out, especially the cell-room which hadn't had even a drunken Saturday-night-cowboy in it for a couple of months now. It faced the east, faced the roadway, and dust from out there came in and settled until it got so thick he had to use a broom to get rid of most of it.

Once, someone had suggested nailing cotton over the high little barred windows. He hadn't done this and now, as he entered the cool old building he thought of it again. But hell it would cause talk — Craig Stanton was even too lazy to dung out his cell-room, folks would say.

He tossed down his hat thinking he might be getting a little too sensitive to what people thought about his job.

That lanky man down the road dropped his smoke and crossed to the general store to buy some sacked tobacco and wheat-straw cigarette papers. There were some women at the dry-goods counter so he had to wait until the vinegary-faced storekeeper got around to waiting on him.

He studied the store's gloomy and deep interior, the location of counters and other things, the location of that big iron safe beyond the dozing old man with the sleeve-protectors, who reminded him of his grandfather back in Kansas.

Jasper had already told him where the safe was. How perfectly it was located for what they had in mind. What eventually stuck in John's mind was how the hell they were going to get that thing open if the storekeeper refused, even at the risk of his life, to open it for them.

He saw the old man's head nod and turned to slowly watch. Then he smiled, and when Caleb came over to toss down the sack of tobacco and the packet of papers, he was still smiling. Caleb thought he was being friendly and nodded briskly without returning the smile. This was the second one of those unshaven, unwashed saddle-tramps he'd had this morning; maybe the outfits were hiring again.

Outside, John saw a cloud of dust coming lazily from those little narrow, high barred windows across at the jailhouse. He rolled a smoke he felt no need for, guessed someone over there was cleaning house, lit up and turned to walk southward toward the livery-barn where Jasper and the dayman were in casual discussion of the price of horseflesh.

Some years it was good, and for a fact, as

the dayman expostulated, some seasons of the year a man could get nearly twice as much for a using horse as he could get other times.

Winter was the poorest time. Even the cow outfits did precious little riding-out when it was ten or twenty below zero with ice atop snowdrifts five feet high, and around town folks did not even think in terms of horseflesh. No one wanted to buy a horse when all they could do for three or four months was fork hay into him.

It was all true. Jasper sympathised. He even said he and his partner had dealt in horseflesh a time or two. He did not say that they had never failed to make money at it, and under no circumstances would he ever have said how they had managed to do that.

It was a lazy afternoon, heat built up, people complained a little, saying generally that it was too early for heat and their blood had not been able to thin down from winter yet.

Caleb Hotchkiss did a little business in sulphur and molasses. Mothers dosed their young ones with a tablespoon of that mixture every springtime to get the blood down thin enough so heat wouldn't bring on croup and the summer-complaint.

At the liverybarn, which had a wide, dirt-floored long runway from in front straight through out back to the rear alleyway, it would remain ten degrees cooler inside than outside all summer long. Later, starting about mid-July, old men would give up their benches on the east side of the road out front of the stores where they soaked up early-springtime sunshine, and amble down to hover in the liverybarn runway to do their whittling, quiet talking, and tobacco-juice spraying in cool and gloomy shade.

Cutler had its seasonal routines like every other town in the territory, and they were just about all the same until a person reached one of the cities such as Cheyenne or Fort Laramie, or one of the railroad towns at the sidings, but Long Grass Valley was distant from any of those places. In fact most of the inhabitants of Long Grass Valley had never been to those cities and the ones which had, had returned complaining and swearing they would never visit another city where there was so much noise and folks were always in a hurry, and if you asked a stranger the time of day he'd scowl and hurry on his way.

As the dayman told Jasper, he had come from Laramie to get away from all that. A place that had more than five thousand people all together was just plain not natural.

He also mentioned in their discussion that Wayman's Rafter W outfit would be fetching in thirty geldings to the public corrals sometime tomorrow and the buyer had already paid the liveryman for an overnight bait of hay, then he was going to head south with the geldings the following morning. "More cash in town," the hostler had said, with a wise wink at Jasper. "My boss says that's what we got to have to keep the town thrivin', and he'd ought to know. Him and the feller who runs the general store — cantankerous bastard he is — are the biggest businessmen in Cutler."

Jasper smiled. "They'd ought to keep that old safe at the store plumb full of money, then."

The dayman winked again, slyly this time. "They been stuffin' money into that darned iron box year in and year out ever since I been around here — four years now. So have them cowmen out across the valley. Must be maybe even ten thousand dollars in there by now?"

"How much?"

"Well; I'm only guessin' you got to understand. Hell, I never even seen inside. But they sure got plenty of money in the safe even if it ain't really that much."

Ten thousand dollars was the highest figure the liverybarn dayman could even imagine. He worked for three dollars a month and got to sleep on horseblankets in the harness-room free.

"They got it stuffed full, I'll bet you. Maybe some folks bury their money in tomato tins in the ground, but I've heard plenty of gossip about that safe being chock full, and seems to me it's got to be."

Jasper offered the dayman a chew, waited until the other man had bitten off his cheekful and returned the plug, then said, "Best me and my partner can do is sleep another night in your loft and ride out tomorrow lookin' for work. I can't imagine havin' so much money I'd have to stuff it in an iron box."

The dayman was sympathetic. "Yeah, I know all about that. Me, I never had enough money to do much with neither. Not even when I was breakin' colts for cow outfits — until I got jumped off in some rocks one time and hurt my back and couldn't ride much any more." He swung an arm. "Now I'm down to this — three gawdamned dollars and beddin' a month." He let the arm drop dejectedly. "Well hell, I better get to work. If the boss comes along and catches me loafin' I won't even have that."

Jasper sighed in pity and watched the day-man go limping away.

The afternoon was waning, there were shadows along the roadway and under the overhangs on the west side of town. He ambled up front and saw John strolling down toward him.

7

HALF A MOON

"That old gaffer back there with the sleeve-socks on his forearms is the answer," John explained as they loped easily southeasterly in the rising warmth of another fresh day.

"If that storekeeper won't open it the old man will. And the box is back where we won't even have to hang no blanket over the roadside window. Jasper, it looks good to me."

It had also looked good to Jasper, but after his discussion with the dayman at the barn he had been thinking almost entirely of the wealth behind that steel door with the scarlet sunset painted on its front.

"Could be as much as ten thousand dollars in there," he told John Hall. "Well, that's a guess; I don't reckon anyone'd really know but the storekeeper and that old duffer. But I was told folks been stuffin' their money in there for years."

"Maybe more'n ten thousand, then,"

exclaimed John, with a wide smile. "Gawd-dammit, Jas, why didn't we think of this long ago, before we shagged our butts all over creation with horses and cattle?"

The answer was not as simple to give as it might have been, and in fact Jasper was not interested in making the attempt. He said, "That feller who owns Rafter W is bringin' in thirty head of geldings today to leave overnight at the public corrals."

John began to faintly frown. "Then why in hell are we ridin' down here when we'd ought to be ridin' northwest, up where them loose horses are so's we can take our pick without no one being around?"

"Because *I* like to pick the times and the places, and not be stampeded into anything," replied methodical and cautious Jasper White. "Don't worry about the horses; when we're ready we'll pick us out the pair we want."

"When, damn it?"

Jasper curbed a short answer. This was his partner's particular shortcoming; he was always impatient, always quick to jump at things. "Maybe when we're finished lookin' the town over; maybe tomorrow night we'll head back up to the bluff and strike camp. Pick out the horses day after tomorrow, then ride down here again about Saturday. Seems to me they do their biggest business in these cow-towns on Saturday. And Saturday afternoon — in the early evenin' when folks are at home havin' supper and gettin' ready for Saturday night at the saloon — we'll walk in on the storekeeper."

John rode a while in thoughtful silence, then heaved a sigh as though in grudging agreement, and under the gaze of the older man, he finally said, "All right. Did you figure out anything about the town marshal?"

"Loafs at the harness works some of the time. Visits around town. I never once saw him enter the saloon, and that's sort of strange. Never in my life knew a lawman who didn't drink — at least a little. Anyway, he looks sort of big and punky and lazy to me. I was talkin' with that feller runs the stage office. He said the marshal's a nice feller who's likely never done an honest day's work in his whole life."

John listened with the expression of a man who was having a private judgment confirmed. "That's the way he struck me too. All the same, we got to know where he'll be when we're inside the store."

"Eatin' supper," stated Jasper, and stood in his stirrups to watch some distant dust. "I kept tabs on him last night from out front of the liverybarn. He heads for supper with the first swarm of fellers from around town who like to eat early. I'll watch him again tonight." Jasper sank down and pointed. "Cattle drive," he said, and joined with his partner in watching the distant cloud of rising dust grow and move and fade far back as men herded a large band of cattle almost due northward. It was too early to be making a gather for a drive down to rails-end, so that had to be a riding crew taking a herd to someone's marking ground, which would be about right for this early time of the season. It was best to get the ear-marking, castrating and branding done before fly-time, otherwise cursing rangeriders had to do an extra job, and one they usually despised — fetching in fly-blown big calves to up-end and scrape free of maggots.

At a small creek the pair of outlaws halted to drink and water their horses, then to sit a while in leafy willow shade doing nothing, just lying back enjoying sunlight and fragrant early summer warmth.

Later, with the afternoon advancing, they took their time about riding back and did not reach Cutler until shortly before the dayman at the liverybarn headed for his nightly session at the saloon when the nightman came in.

They cared for their own horses and split up out front, John heading for the cafe, Jasper shambling along in his stooped way for the saloon, where he and the dayman shared one, then the dayman left and Jasper talked with the barman until he thought it was close enough, and walked out front to bite off a fresh chew and loaf, watching the front of the second brick building in town.

Craig was over there listening to the lamentations of a carpenter named Swenson whose neat stack of pine boards out back of the shed where he made coffins, had been stolen, right down to the pair of sawhorses they had been stacked upon.

Craig promised to look into it. After the carpenter had left he said, "Those damned squatters," and grabbed his hat to hike across the road for supper.

Ever since the first trickle of settlers had appeared thefts around town had increased. Mainly, they stole boards and nails, pieces of tin for roofs, shovels and picks, things they had no money to pay for but which they could not survive without, and while he understood their predicament, and to some extent, at any rate, sympathised with them, his heart had been hardening against those people the last year or so. It seemed there was no such thing as a squatter who would not steal.

At the cafe there were five other towns-men, and that lanky, unshorn, faded rangerider Craig had seen around town the past day or two. He nodded and sank down to wait. There was no such thing as choice of foods except for breakfast. Supper was something the cafeman concocted out of what was available and while this should have brought wrath down upon his head, it rarely did because he was an outstanding cook. He had to be; his looks were unpleas-ant and his disposition was even worse.

That faded cowboy bolted his food, dropped coins and arose, heading for the door. Marshal Stanton scarcely heeded his departure, but the cowboy turned at the door to look back as though he expected the lawman to be staring at him. Reassured, he eased the door closed, looked up at the front of the saloon, then hiked in the op-posite direction. The watcher up there smiled to himself and ambled down to the cafe to have supper.

He had barely received his platter when the lawman also departed. More men en-tered, the later diners, one of which was the harness-maker. He and Craig met at the door and the harness-maker dourly said, "The saddle's just about finished. Come up tomorrow and see what it looks like."

Craig agreed and paused to look north and south out of long habit, then, although he normally could have crossed over to lock up the jailhouse for the night, he heard squealing horses down in the vicinity of the public corral and went down there.

Jess Wayman and his riders were leaning in the poor light gazing in at the geldings. When Craig Stanton came up Jeff turned and nodded. Wayman's riders chose this moment to head for the cafe. A supper in town was a rarity.

That disreputable-looking tall rangeman was down at the far end of the corral also looking at the geldings, but if he noticed the lawman and the rancher he gave no sign of it.

Jeff said, "Thirty head," and Craig nodded. He had heard of this drive. The animals were quality; none were smooth-mouthed yet, a thing any experienced horseman could discern even in poor light without getting inside to mouth them.

"You raise fine stock," he told Jeff Wayman. "If I ever get a dollar a head I'll come out."

Wayman smiled. "Take more than one dollar, Marshal, but come out anyway." He looked toward the roadway. "I'm supposed

90

to meet the buyer here at six."

"You got half an hour to wait," stated Stanton, who had just left the cafe and had seen the clock over the counter. "Get a fair price? You should have. Those look like fine animals."

Wayman leaned, gazing in at his sleek animals. "A fair price," he assented. "I expect a man never gets as much as he figures he should for animals like these though. On the other hand, I got more horses now than my grass'll stand. Held back year before last because the market went to hell. Now I've got two-year-olds all over the place. Had to move my best loose-stock up close to the sandstone bluff to make room down south for the young horses."

The lanky, faded rangeman straightened and turned to amble over in the direction of the alley entrance to the dimly lighted livery-barn runway. He did not enter, but leaned out back making a smoke, hat punched back, long, strong body loose as he lit up and blew smoke at the first pale stars of early evening.

Later, he got a drink of water at the trough, killed his smoke and entered the barn. There was no one in sight so he went up the nailed slats which served as a loft-ladder, got into the pitch darkness up there, kicked some hay around, tossed down his hat and was shaking out of his boots when Jasper came up through the crawl hole to say, "You here, John?"

It got dark in the loft before it got dark anywhere else. There was one loft door, back on the alleyside, and it was tightly closed.

John grunted, and as his partner came through the loose hay he said, "Wayman still down there at the corrals?"

"No. Him and some feller with a big black moustache was out front though. Why?"

"He just told the lawman he'd put his best horses up at the base of the cliff. Crowded for room and had to run them up there."

Jasper sank down with a rattling sigh. "Is that so? Well sir, things is workin' in our favour. The marshal had supper just like always." Jasper swore at pulling off his boots. Lately, his feet seemed to swell more than they ever had before, along toward the end of the day. When he tossed aside the last boot he lay back in the fragrant, yielding straw. "We can ride out before sunup, John, and start things moving."

The younger man smiled in the darkness. "I'm ready. Did you hear any more talk about how much money they got in that iron safe?"

"No. But it's not worryin' me. It'll be plenty."

"Yeah. You didn't happen to fetch back a pony of whisky, by any chance?"

"No. And you better sleep if we're goin' out of here before sunup."

Jasper burrowed deep, scratched briefly, then composed himself for sleep. That was something; lately he seemed to want to sleep a little more than he had in times past.

Outside, the town settled in for a pleasant night. The moon was half full, the stars were as bright as new-blown opaque glass, and the chill which normally should have been arriving about now, seemed to be holding off. Late springtime and early summer mingled this late in the early year; it was even possible that, excluding the rains sure to come now and then over the next month or so, they might continue to have warm nights as well as bell-clear pleasant days.

But that was something a man never wanted to bet his money on; not in Wyoming anyway.

8
THE RIDERS

The early morning was not as cold as Jasper had expected it to be, but it was dark when he and John walked their horses quietly out of Cutler on a northwesterly course, so not until an hour and a half later, when there was a pale grey dullness along the saw-toothed horizon did they have decent enough visibility to see why it was warm.

The sky was slightly overcast. There was one of those veil-like misty high shrouds blanketing the heavens, and although fading stars were visible through it they looked obscure and fuzzy.

John said, "Good. It'll maybe rain tonight or tomorrow, and that's going to wash out our tracks."

Jasper said nothing. He was worrying his first cud for the day. It was never quite the same as breakfast but over the years he had more than once had to use it as a substitute, and he was not too upset. Anyway, they had grub at the cliff-top camp.

As for rainfall, he'd ridden through his share of that too, and as John had observed, it was about as much help as it was hindrance. His slicker was up at the cliff-top camp too. Providing he could get that before rain commenced he would not mind a little downpour.

When there was a high overcast the world always seemed to sleep-in a little longer. Even horses and cattle remained in their beds. Once, a small band of horses spooked at the scent of riders but it only ran a dozen or so yards then halted, more curious than fearful, but in the weak light all they could make out was two lumpy moving figures east of them, and riding northward.

The day was close to arriving by the time they were a third of the way. It was brightening with a strong taint of reflected-upward light from the sun beyond high mountains by the time they were well into Rafter W range, and by the time they loped into the foothills across an empty land, even the sun was climbing.

It was a long ride but they had made good time, had utilised the foothills as quickly as they could, moving out of habit with the stealth of wolves, especially after sunlight came.

That overcast got burned through but it did not entirely dissipate, another sign a rain was on its way even though the only clouds were a few fleecy shapes hanging directly above the farthest rims.

At the cliff-camp Jasper swung off first. Now that he was satisfied that they should move, he was quick and precise in his movements.

It took only moments for them to strike camp, lash tight, professional blanket-rolls aft of cantles, fill saddlebags and look around before mounting to head back down, and even though they were not much worried over the prospect of detection, since they had seen Jeff Wayman's personal mount and the mounts of his riders still in the public corrals before riding out this morning, they nevertheless moved carefully as they left the cliff-top for the last time, angling away from the brakes below in search of loose-stock.

Here too, they were favoured.

There was a seepage spring up a slot-kind of canyon. A band had nighted there and some, perhaps half the band, was still up there picking at grass and browse when the outlaws saw them and moved instantly into position without consulting, much the same way hunting wolves moved, one to block the mouth of the little canyon, the other one to take down his rope and ride slowly, almost indifferently, up where the loose-stock finally saw him emerge from a thicket of underbrush.

Unbroke horses probably would have lunged up the canyon walls cutting and scratching themselves in a frantic effort to break clear, but these were well-broke, powerfully-muscled, using horses. If there were colts among them, or even heavy mares, John did not see them as he halted, exchanging glances with the motionless horses.

There were at least thirty head in this bunch. Maybe more farther back through a screen of thorny thicket where the spring was. Two horses in particular appealed to John. Both were bays, big, stout, strong animals in their prime. He smiled, scratched his ribs, snugged up his gloves and started to shake out a small loop. One of the bays turned with an intelligent eye and took several steps forward. John halted movement, watched, and when the horse showed no fear John spoke to him softly in a gentle, deep tone. The bay dropped his head and started cropping grass and John said, "I'll be damned." Not so much because the horse was gentle and tractable, but because this was going to be too easy.

He swung off, looped his reins in the brush and walked right up to the horse, slowly, talking his way up. When he was close enough the horse lifted its calm eyes, brought its handsome head around and allowed itself to be caught without so much as a tremor.

John kept shaking his head; it was like catching some kid's old pony. He led the horse back to his own mount and started to make the change.

Jasper appeared farther back, curious about what was taking so long; why there had been no wild charge down the canyon past John when he went in rope swinging. John grinned and pointed. "See if you can talk your way up to that other one."

Jasper probably would not have been this fortunate but for the fact that since John had done nothing to frighten them, the other horses were still calm and interested. But the second big handsome bay rocked back and rolled his eyes, even snorted softly as Jasper walked in close, and had to halt a moment before the bay would ease up a little, stand like stone while he too was captured the same way. Jasper shook his head, but he said nothing as he led the second big bay back where his watching

98

horse showed curiosity about what was going on.

When they finally rode back down out of the canyon they were stared at by the pair of horses they had abandoned. Then these two animals went back to smell noses, and squeal a little at their new acquaintances.

John's bay was as honest as he was good. Jasper's bay had a tendency to shy a little but otherwise he showed no bad habits as the pair of men reined back and forth throughout the foothills, taking the same stealthy trail back in the general direction of Cutler that they had used earlier.

John looped his reins and rolled a smoke and smiled. He hadn't covered three miles before he and his stolen horse had achieved a perfect understanding. John said, "I didn't like the idea of leavin' my horse back there. A hunnert dollars is a lot of money to just walk off from. But by gawd this was a good trade."

Jasper, however, did not slack off on his wary watchfulness. After his new mount had shied twice, once at a bird exploding from a bush as they rode past, and again when they startled a long-legged big brush-rabbit, Jasper said, "This son of a bitch is just naturally spooky, or he's got weak eyesight."

But Jasper's horse manifested no other

bad characteristics. He neither offered to pitch nor run and he was very light on the reins. "Sure as hell was broke right," the older man eventually admitted, relaxing from his deep seat in the saddle.

They had mid-morning warmth shading off into early afternoon heat on their ride back, nor did they hasten. As Jasper saw it, even if Jeff Wayman and his riding crew had left town homeward bound after breakfast, having delivered their horses to the buyer, because the outlaws were holding to a due-easterly course there was almost no chance of an encounter.

They did not in fact see any riders at all and they kept watch all the way over to the stageroad where they turned southward, finally, in almost the exact place where they had reached the road on their first ride down toward town. In fact they saw nothing except a morning stage, north-bound, and they left the road to give it plenty of room, and to avoid the inevitable pall of dust in its wake.

But the mistiness overhead seemed to be increasing by late afternoon, when they were still ten or twelve miles from Cutler, and that gave them something to consider because Mother Nature was absolutely indifferent to the plans of humans; she would dump rain or sometimes even freak snow-storms on weddings or burials, or even bank robberies, with complete blind indifference, which was something Jasper White and John Hall accepted as a matter of course whether it fitted their private plans or not, and they made whatever corrections and changes Nature's moods required them to make.

But the clouds had not appreciably increased even though they had advanced down from the rims and were now lying above the rearward cliff. Jasper gave all this judicious consideration before giving his opinion of it.

"Them clouds got to fill up and get a hell of a lot darker and fuller before it rains. . . . Maybe early tomorrow morning."

After the providential good fortune up that little seepage-spring canyon John was viewing everything as favourable, so he indifferently glanced upwards and around, then shrugged. "If it rains hard enough tomorrow morning we'd ought to be twenty miles or more from Cutler, and like I said, all it'll do is clean out our sign."

Jasper left off considering the weather and turned his full attention to oncoming roof-tops. They had to be at the general store before the storekeeper locked up and went home for the night. This kind of enterprise was not like driving off a band of horses or cattle; it required much closer timing.

Until they were only a short distance from Cutler there was no more conversation, but as they swerved to reach the east side of town, heading off where a stand of trees guarded a nearby creek, Jasper said, "We got back just about right."

They left the Rafter W horses tied out of sight, did not loosen *cinchas* which rangemen normally did if they expected the animals to have to wait for any length of time, and made certain the animals could not move much nor get their heads down to the ground. When they returned they did not expect to be pursued nor to be in a desperate hurry, but on the other hand, they could be sure of nothing. If they happened to need these horses fast, there would be no time to snug up girths.

Cutler was shading off from afternoon toward evening. Here and there people had lighted lamps although there was no actual darkness yet and would not be for another hour or more, but not all homes and stores were blessed with windows facing the directions which caught the last sunlight.

Jasper walked slowly, his stoop more pronounced when he moved like this, and once he turned to say, "Be better if folks didn't see us. Right now, I'd say the liverybarn-fellers figure we got hired on, or maybe give it up and rode away. That'll help."

John was agreeable. When they came over to the east-side alley and hovered near a sagging old rotting pole fence, they halted. The rear of buildings dead ahead looked disreputable, even in poor and fading daylight. The alley was a litter of discards but the aroma which reached them was from the cafe and it made Jasper sigh, then automatically fish out his plug of tobacco.

The town was quiet. For men who did not carry pocket-watches the outlaws had made good time back and had seemed to be in place at the exact moment when they should have been.

Jasper spat, listening to the little homely sounds, while John shifted position in his impatience. This was the one thing which annoyed him particularly about his partner. When John was ready to strike he never viewed delays caused by extreme caution with even a little patience. On the other hand, he understood why Jasper was like this and over the past few years he could not honestly say Jasper had ever miscalculated.

Jasper shifted his cud, finally, which seemed to presage something, then he reached to tug loose the tie-down over his Colt-handle, and sidled out of shadows along the rotting old fence heading southward down the alleyway. When they were directly behind the general store he looked at the barred windows, shook his head in disapproval and said softly, "That bastard don't trust no one."

John smiled and paced along soundlessly until they reached the end of the alley and would have turned right to reach the main roadway except that a young man holding on to the hand of a voluptuous young woman came strolling, both mindful of nothing on this earth but each other as they walked purposefully eastward towards the darkening open country beyond town where it was possible to be alone.

The pair of outlaws had to fade back and merge with alley darkness until the lovers had passed and Jasper made a bleak remark about those two, until he was able to step out again and look after them, then turn and make certain there would be no more strollers.

They had no difficulty reaching the corner of the main roadway where it junctured with the side-road those lovers had disappeared down.

John smiled. "Not a darn soul."

It was true. Up as far as they could see the roadway and both plankwalks were empty. Jasper spat again and bobbed his head. "Now, if that damned constable's at supper," he murmured, and lifted a booted foot to the walkway heading northward in the direction of the general store.

There were several lights now, among the stores. As soon as the final customers of the day were disposed of, merchants would douse their lights, lock up and head for home.

The light inside the general store was near the counter along the north wall where Caleb Hotchkiss had his main cash drawer.

Through the southernmost edge of the roadway window Jasper saw the merchant stuffing something into a soiled little flour sack. Leaning in idle discussion while the storekeeper did this, was the town marshal, his broad back to the window.

Jasper said, "Gawddammit!"

They waited, nerves beginning to crawl. Jasper had been sure the lawman would be up at the cafe. Instead, the big loafer was slouching in there talking to the storekeeper.

John, with a hand on the stock of his holstered Colt was less perturbed, and when

Craig Stanton continued to lean and idly talk, his back to the roadway, John finally said, "What the hell's the difference; we can knock him over the head too. One skull or two — it don't matter."

Jasper neither moved nor spoke. He had ceased to masticate, too. Once, he cast a worried look up the roadway where sound carried softly from the far upper end of town. Three horsemen were jogging in from the east, turning as they reached the road to haul down and walk their mounts to the rack out front of the saloon. They wasted little time tying up and stamping over the wooden walk to enter where the only really bright lights were now showing.

Craig shoved upright off the counter and stood watching Caleb walk briskly back to pitch his money-sack atop the counter where the old man was doggedly waiting. It was something they did every night. The old man climbed off his padded stool and took the sack to the safe. As he bent, all the watchers from the roadway could make out was his thin, long back.

Craig and the storekeeper exchanged a few words then the lawman turned, taking his time as he crossed to the doorway.

Jasper elbowed his partner. They retreated as far as a smelly dog-trot between buildings, stepped in there and waited. When the footfalls of the lawman faded northward they stepped out again.

This was the moment they had been particularly waiting for. There were only two people in the general store, both of whom knew the combination to the steel safe. Within moments Caleb Hotchkiss would lock up and walk home, and the old man from back by the 'bank' would no doubt do the same. They knew the storekeeper's name but had no idea who the shuffling old gaffer back there with the sleeve-protectors, was. Nor did it matter.

Jasper paused until John was about to elbow him, then moved ahead, stooped, but now his peculiar stance did not seem as if the burden of years had bowed him, now it more nearly resembled the head-thrust and shoulder-thrust of a vulture, and that was exactly what it was and had always been.

9

THE INTRUSION

Old Frank was turning back after twirling the knob of the safe and saw the rough pair of unshaven men enter. Caleb had his back to the door dourly refolding bolt goods which female shoppers had run through their fingers, leaving them in disarray. He did not know anyone had come in from the roadway until old Frank cleared his throat.

The stooped man Caleb recognised at once, and he thought he remembered selling tobacco to the other one, but as he turned upon the point of saying the store was closed, the younger one drew and the stooped older man reached around to close and bolt the roadside door.

Caleb could hardly breathe. He knew what was happening but it had never happened before. His father told him once, years ago, of the robbery they'd had, and that time four outlaws had died between the storefront and the north end of town.

Old Frank leaned, his rheumy eyes gently widening. It had taken little the past few years to confuse the old man, but fifty years ago he would have responded to this situation with an explosion of action, and some remnants of those days lingered. He started to reach for the dusty scattergun beneath his counter. Until this evening he had not touched that sawed-off twelve-gauge even to clean it, in five years.

The older man turned back from the door and palmed his sixgun, stepped around the taller outlaw and aimed squarely at old Frank as he advanced toward the rear of the store.

"Put your hand back atop the counter," he ordered, and cocked the Colt.

Confusion came over the old man. He stared at Jasper rather than at the cocked Colt and he did not bring his hand up. He had a grip under there on the shotgun.

Jasper swore at him and gestured with the cocked gun. "Get it up, you old bastard! Put that other hand atop the counter!"

Caleb turned just his head. It had been a source of exasperation with him for a long while now, how old Frank got upset and baffled by simple things. But he knew what was happening now, which neither of the gunmen could possibly know. Caleb said,

"Leave it be, Frank. Do like he told you —
put both hands on the countertop."

The old man obeyed the same way an old
dog might have; he responded to a familiar
voice, and slowly lifted his hand and sank it
gently beside the other blue-veined hand.
But his eyes did not leave Jasper's face.

John wig-wagged toward Caleb Hotchkiss.
"Get over there, mister, and open the safe.
An' if you got a gun in there I'll blow your
lousy brains all over the wall when you
reach for it. *Move!* Shag your butt back
there!"

Jasper was already behind the counter. He
pushed old Frank, pushed him again and
lined him against the dark rear wall where
the old man stood on frail legs, his eyes
beginning to water, his mouth to tremble.

When John herded the storekeeper back
there the four of them were too far from the
one lamp up on the counter near the cash
drawer to be seen unless someone out front
stood and waited, then caught motion and
movement in the deeper back-wall gloom
and shadows.

Jasper ignored old Frank to study Caleb
Hotchkiss, nearly a head taller; in fact
Hotchkiss was even taller than John, who
was not a short man. Jasper said, "Open it,
storekeeper," and pushed his gun-muzzle

softly against Caleb's body. "Otherwise we'll wire it with blasting powder and tie you and the old duffer to it. . . . You got a couple of seconds to make up your mind." Jasper shoved the gun, gently.

John let his gun sag. Neither the old watery-eyed gaffer against the wall nor the ashen storekeeper left him feeling anything but scorn for his adversaries. For those two he did not even need a gun. A fist would double them both over, or a slash across the back of the head with a Colt-barrel.

"You ain't got all night," he said sharply, watching Caleb Hotchkiss.

Jasper explained it for Caleb. "You don't open it, the old bastard will, and if *he* does, I'm going to kill you, storekeeper."

Caleb cast an agonised look over where the old man was sniffling a little, his legs, which had tremors if he remained standing too long, beginning to shake slightly. Caleb stepped heavily ahead and sank to one knee. His hand shook as he lifted it to the knob.

John smiled. Right from the beginning this has gone so well, so perfectly in fact, he could scarcely believe their good fortune. He turned, saw the sawed-off shotgun beneath the counter and leathered his Colt as he stepped up, lifted the gun and swung back, holding it in both hands. At close range there was no more gorily lethal firearm than a short-barrelled scattergun, especially one of big-gauge.

But he did not need it.

Caleb fumbled on the first try and had to spin the dial to begin anew. Jasper leaned, shaking his head as though he were a teacher and Caleb Hotchkiss a pupil. "Slow down, damn it, and get hold of yourself, storekeeper." He did not raise his voice. "Not a damned thing'll happen if you just open the box and mind your manners. Now commence again — and slow down."

Caleb ran a soiled sleeve under his nose and across his mouth, pushed both palms down his trouser-legs and settled back gazing at the door and the knob. He looked up at Jasper. "Let me give you my money from in there, and for gawd's sake leave the rest. Mister, it ain't my money." The storeman's anguish was palpable enough so that even John felt it. John answered almost smiling. "Ain't our money neither, storekeeper, but it will be directly. Just get the gawd-damned door open."

John hauled back one hammer of the shotgun and Caleb half twisted to gaze over his shoulder. Those two big-bore muzzles were less than eight feet from his head. He turned back, dried his hands and started again.

Jasper shifted the Colt, drew out his plug, bit off a ragged corner, returned the plug to his pocket and put the gun back in his right hand.

Outside, up the roadway somewhere a dog began barking and a pair of horsemen loped into town, one of them teasing the dog by cupping both hands and imitating a bitch-coyote. The dog went into a frenzy and men's loud laughter came down into the tense silence of the store.

Caleb had sweat on his long, narrow face and old Frank was leaning to try and prevent his palsied legs from shaking so noticeably.

Jasper had not looked at his partner since they had got back there, and now as he sensed the door would shortly open he also ignored old Frank. It was as though only he and Caleb Hotchkiss were in the store — in the whole damned world for that matter.

The door yielded. Caleb arose to a stoop and leaned to swing it back.

Inside, the sixgun was lying upon the top shelf. Jasper reached, tossed the gun across the floor in the direction of the desk and finally glanced back. John still had one hammer of the scattergun back. Jasper winked at his partner and leaned.

There were pouches in there, with names in black ink on each one. There were also some thick brown envelopes, and in a steel drawer lay bundles of greenbacks tied with string.

Jasper said, "John, look in there."

"Can't see from here. Just load it and let's get on our way."

Jasper kept staring a moment longer, then turned and gave Caleb Hotchkiss a rough shove. "Step back. Keep back there out of the way. You got a flour sack? Never mind." Jasper knelt and used both hands to fill his shirt-front. The pouches were as heavy as lead. Gold was that heavy. In fact in pouches it was heavier than lead so Jasper finished loading himself by stuffing those bundles of green notes inside his shirt.

When he arose he had not taken even half. He pointed and said, "Fill up, John. I'll watch."

But there was no threat. There did not appear to be even the possibility of a threat. Those boisterous rangemen were inside the saloon now, probably being just as noisy, but it could not be heard this far distant.

The younger outlaw moved more precisely, more quickly. Nor did he seem to mind the dead weight as he shoved pouches inside his shirt and used the other hand to stuff in those small bales of greenbacks.

The safe held neat stacks of paper but neither Jasper nor John even glanced at them. It also held some ledgers, and when John came to the small, soiled flour-sack which was not even half full, he turned with a short laugh and flung it at the storekeeper. "Ain't enough to bother with, and you'll need it to open up with in the morning."

Caleb caught his little sack with both hands, more in a defensive gesture than because he wanted to catch it particularly.

The shock was past. He clutched the sack watching John, and he said, "It don't belong to me by even half. That's the savings of two-thirds of the folks around Long Grass Valley. The cowmen, mostly, and folks here in town. You're takin' what they been savin' for years."

Jasper finished shoving lumps around inside his shirt and looked at the store-keeper, whose stricken face matched his tone of voice.

"We're gamblers, mister," he told Hotch-kiss. "We lay our necks on the line and you folks are bettin' your savings we'll lose." Jasper smiled at the storekeeper. "Right now, I'd say we're goin' to win."

Caleb looked at Jasper with the expression

of a man who could not find words. His mouth was open, his eyes were dark with anguish. He turned slowly as John arose trying to shove more of those little pouches into trouser-pockets, but having trouble.

"They'll never stop hunting you," Caleb said, in a fading tone which did not inspire much belief. "You'll never be able to make off and get free."

Old Frank flickered rheumy eyes from the back-wall. "Me too, Cal," he said. "Me too — I got to pee."

Jasper and John gazed at old Frank, just for a moment of uncomfortable premonition; it had to happen about like that to every man who lived into the very late years. Jasper turned and said, "Anything left?" John shook his head. "Then let's get along." John had the sawed off riot-gun cradled in his arm. Both of them looked, and moved, as though they were fat and unwieldy.

Jasper looked at Hotchkiss, then flicked a glance back where the old man was unsteadily leaning, and brought his gaze back to Hotchkiss. He knew what he had said they must do, but right now it seemed like a waste of time. Furthermore it was difficult to bend over and straighten up. He caught John's glance and the younger man moved towards Caleb Hotchkiss, whose eyes wid-

116

ened until the whites showed. He threw up an arm but not swiftly enough. John dropped him with a blow across the top of the head and as Hotchkiss tumbled, struck and rolled limply the old man bleated, eyes darting like those of a cornered animal.

John turned toward him but Jasper said, "That's all right. Come on. We'll head out the back way."

John did not move. "You can't leave this old bastard."

"Yes you can. He don't know up from down. Now come along." Jasper hastened to the dark corridor and did not look back. His partner glanced twice back and forth, then said something under his breath and hurried into the corridor, still carrying the sawed-off scattergun.

The rear door had three bolts and as Jasper swore his way through, opening one after the other, he said, "That louse plain didn't have no trust in anyone at all. Not only three bolts but the back of the damned door's been plated with steel."

The door opened finally, and they stepped out. It had not been noticeably warm inside but it must have been, because now they instantly felt cold air in their faces. Now, too, the saloon-noise was discernible as they fled across the alleyway and reached the gate in that punky old rotten log fence.

Behind them someone fired a handgun from just inside a doorway; the sound was as loud as a cannon, compressed like that, and Jasper dropped to one knee as he whirled to fire back. John yelled at him, "That old son of a bitch!" and whatever else he said was lost in the noise as Jasper aimed at the dark doorway and fired back. Then he jumped up swearing and running. They could not hear the noise from the saloon and as they lumbered, laden with money pouches, sucking down big lungsful of air, John bitterly said, "So that old bastard was harmless was he? Picked up the safe-gun off the floor is what he did."

Jasper was upset enough to say nothing even after they reached the horses, tugged loose and heavily loaded themselves up across leather.

They rode back through the trees, splashed across that little watercourse which ran in among the timber, and emerged on the far side where Jasper held aloft a hand to halt and listen.

There was noise back there, but it sounded faint, and it could have been coming from the saloon rather than from some excited men down at the store, there was no sensible way to determine which.

118

John jerked the Rafter W horse around with his reinhand, holding aloft the scatter-gun in his other hand. He did not even admonish Jasper to hurry along with him, he simply hooked the bay horse.

The smell of rain was strong, the nearly full horsethief's moon was opaque and fuzzy up there, and only the strongest stars could show through the increasing overcast. It would rain, perhaps as Jasper had thought, just before dawn tomorrow.

They covered five miles before easing off to conserve horse-strength, and as they walked along, still westerly, Jasper swore. He was as disgusted with himself, for his own mistakes, as he was with anything else, and yet, as he tried to convince himself, even if they had lost their best advantage, they still had the second-best one working for them: the darkness.

John's resentment passed too, after they had covered another mile or two. He twisted to stand in his stirrups but there was nothing to be seen nor heard back yonder. As he eased down the last time he made a philosophical observation.

"Well hell; it couldn't *all* go our way. An' the main thing is we got it." He patted his lumpy upper body.

Jasper was one of those people whose

moods lasted longer. He was dour and unforgiving, even to himself, until John said he thought it had to be close to midnight, then they turned southward to start their real rush to escape.

10
RAIN

They piled off just before the light drizzle started, dropped down tiredly in some short grass near a stand of spindly trees and John immediately began fishing forth the small bales of banknotes and the pouches of gold coins.

"Damned stuff must weigh nearly a hunnert pounds," he said, and wasted one moment scanning the sky before opening the choke-cord of one little sack and gently tilting it until coins as dull as ancient copper filled his palm.

"Chris'sake," he breathed, and ignored Jasper who was simply leaning back, eyes half closed, resting his body.

John did not count the gold coins, he eased them gently back, pulled the pucker-string and read the name on the pouch. "J. Wayman. Hey Jas, this here is the money that horserancher got for them geldings yesterday." John laughed. "He worked his tail off raising colts, bringing them through each winter, gettin' them up in top shape to peddle — and by gawd you'n me made the profit. That's *my* kind of ranching." He flicked the tied packets of notes. "You was dead right, Jas. We got enough here to last us a lifetime. Well, a hell of a long time, anyway."

Jasper leaned, watched briefly, then also fished forth one of the little pouches and loosened the throat to trickle coins. His leathery, unshaven, weathered countenance creased a little, but he was tired so as he put the money back, and as he hefted the little sack, all he said was, "It'll be rainin' in another half hour. Let's see how far we can get before then."

The horses were tired and hung in their bits a little, which surprised John Hall. "I thought we was ridin' the best saddlestock in Wyoming," he grumbled and kicked his horse with both heels.

Jasper loped along for another two miles, until the first drizzle commenced, then he halted to untangle the slicker from behind his cantle and shrug into it. He could not get it snapped in front. The gap was at least six inches.

John laughed at him. "You're so rich you can't get around all your money, Jasper."

They walked the horses after that, being far enough from Cutler by this time they did not much fear pursuit. Not until daylight arrived, and by then the rainfall, if it increased a little, would take care of that.

Jasper finally said, "There's nothing wrong with these horses. We're just carryin' too darned much weight. Me, I weigh a hunnert and seventy-five pounds. My rig weighs close to fifty pounds." He paused to look at John. "And I can tell you for a fact I'm carryin' at least a hunnert pounds of gold money. That's more'n a man's got any right to pack on a mule, let alone a horse with a long back and smaller legs."

They continued to walk the horses and John finally became less elated, more silent and solicitous of the horse he was straddling. Privately, he totalled up the weight his animal was carrying. It was also too much for a horse to carry and still make good time with. He twisted to peer back, water dripping from the low front of his curl-brimmed black hat. The land was empty back there.

Westward, the stage road was about two miles distant. It ran arrow-straight across this flat to gently heaving lower range country, due north. Occasionally there were wagon ruts to show where some cow outfit had turned off, but there was no sign of buildings. In fact they did not even see any horses nor cattle until they had been poking along through the steady light drizzle for another hour, with a watery dawn brightening the sombre landscape on all sides, then they came upon some razorbacks and Jasper said, "Hell; I thought folks had quit bothering with them long horned Texas cattle."

John was not the least bit concerned. Not even when a brockle-faced wet cow with a wobbly little calf took a dozen steps in their direction and warningly shook her big rack of horn at them. Jasper had grown up around cattle like this and offered a warning.

"Veer away, that darned old girl's ready to fight."

They got past and the cow returned immediately to her calf, but kept watching them until they were distant enough to no longer pose a threat, then she gave her head a toss and nuzzled her calf.

The land merged out a few miles with the funereal sky. It was one of those drizzly days which were not cold, nor windy, but which had a clamminess which seeped all the way through, even under slickers, to make men feel as old as they were, and in some cases much older.

Its complete melancholy inhibited humour; made men do the minimum which was required of them and do it without a word or even any small sense of accomplishment. For Jasper White it was a day of bleak memories and onward reflections which strove to reach out where there would be sunshine and affluence and comfort — and never quite made it.

He looked at the sky, shook water from his hatbrim and said, "Days like this I almost wish I followed my paw into the blacksmithing business."

John was stuffing a dirty handkerchief inside his shirt where the cadence of his walking mount had made one of the pouches chafe his ribs. "It'll be worth it once we get down where they got railroad cars. We can buy tickets, leave these damned horses, and just set back and ride with our feet up. . . . And get that gallon of whisky."

They halted near noon at an old line-shack which did not appear to have been used in months. There was a woodrat nest in there better than three feet tall, but no sign of its owner and creator.

The horses stood out front with drooping heads, water dripping from their bellies and chins. There was a stove and even some ancient, tinder-dry wood, but it could not safely be used; if anyone saw smoke rising from the tin chimney they might come to investigate. They ate what little food was left, rested an hour then trudged forth, climbed across wet saddle-seats and struck out again.

There was still no sign of pursuit to the north, even though this kind of drizzle did not wash tracks out. Especially on ground which was bone dry to start with. Every droplet was absorbed like wet ink on a blotter, but they were past worrying about that.

Jasper eventually said, "This is just too gawdamned much weight, John. You do what you want to do but first decent hiding place I see I'm going to cache most of mine."

John frowned. "You can't come back for it, Jas. Not for a hell of a long time."

But Jasper knew better. "I've done it before. On a moonless night."

When they reached a shelter of scabby rocks, the only protruding boulders of any size they had encountered so far, Jasper piled off, more stooped than ever, went in among the stones and worked for a half hour making the proper nest in the mud beneath a particular stone, one with lichen, like scabs, on it, hid his fortune, patted mud over the place and sifted gravel atop the mud, then canted several stone slabs with sharp edges to make it all appear perfectly natural. In a couple of hours the drizzle would help this deception.

Then he went back and tiredly hoisted himself back to the saddle, at least seventy-five pounds lighter. As they moved out he watched the bay John was riding. His own horse did not show any immediate reaction to being relieved of all that weight but John's tractable nice big horse seemed to be dragging more and more. In the end, as they came closer to more of those extrusions of what looked to be some ancient form of flinty lava-stone, Jasper said, "We got to find another pair of horses soon now," and his partner bobbed his head, having also been aware the animal under him was wearing down.

But they saw no bands nor any buildings. Once, at a spring where someone had built a stone and mortar water-box, they found recent tracks, but hell, those horses had probably tanked up shortly after sunrise so they could now be ten miles away.

It was a spiral of thin grey smoke beyond a thinly wooded place a mile closer to the roadway which caught Jasper's eye. He drew rein and pointed with a darkly wet glove.

John's spirits rose a little. Wordlessly they turned off in that direction. They were miles from Cutler now; so far in fact they had no apprehension at all even though Jasper kept watch to the rear, and along both sides.

The cabin had been built of those small trees which had evidently once been all around it, and which over the years had been thinned out, not just for the house and corrals but also to supply that stove which had first sent aloft the smoke to attract the outlaws.

They dismounted among the trees, dirty and lumpy and cold-eyed where they stood dripping in their old worn boots, gazing out.

There was no barn, just a small set of holding-corrals to one side, and the cabin, which looked almost square, but which seemed too large for a line-shack. John said, "Squatter, more'n likely."

But what concerned Jasper were those corrals — all empty. "The son of a bitch don't even have a horse," he said bitterly. "Let's go."

They had no alternative so they rode back the way they had come, but angling southward as they got farther from the cabin and the stageroad. It was now past mid-day, the tucked up horses were slow at recovering when they stumbled amid the rocks and in slippery places.

Jasper finally unloaded and trudged ahead leading his animal, ankle-length old black slicker trailing almost in the mud and waving behind where grass-stalks delayed its passage. He walked stooped, head thrust forward, hard, calm eyes fixed upon the southerly foothills which prefaced some larger, thicker but not very high mountains.

John stayed astraddle another mile then he too piled off, transferred most of his little pouches to his saddle bags, and had to discard some personal effects, socks and britches and his only other butternut shirt, to make room.

They walked along about thirty feet apart, leaning into the wind which had not arrived but which they seemed to expect, along with the drizzling rain, even though with this kind of rain there almost never was much wind.

A mile farther on John stopped, breathing hard. He still had about forty pounds of pouched gold coins and paper notes inside his shirt. "I'm plumb tuckered," he said, looking around. "Got to cache some of this dead weight."

They spent an hour finding just the place John sought, and another half hour getting the sacks and greenbacks buried. Afterwards, John tried to roll a smoke but his tobacco was soggy so with a sizzling oath he hurled the sack down and struck out again, leading the worn-down handsome bay horse.

"Why in hell," he finally said to Jasper, "didn't we figure on how *heavy* that much money is?"

Jasper grimaced. "We just didn't, and that's all there is to it. Don't worry; we still own it, and one of these days we'll come back. We're still rich men, John."

That seemed to placate the larger and younger man because as he resumed walking his head was a little higher and his shoulders were squared again. He paused a mile father to look all around, then to shake his head. He had not been looking back for possible pursuit, he was seeking a ranch or maybe a squatter's place where they might be able to steal another pair of mounts.

But the land was empty. That shack back yonder with smoke rising from the stove-pipe was all they encountered.

He saw Jasper watching him and shook off water before saying, "I guess it could be worse. We could have a damned posse right behind," and as if that thought worried him he turned and made a long, sweeping look, then resumed trudging.

Jasper began to wonder about something. "There ain't been enough rain to wash out our marks. Then, how's come there's no chase?"

John had no answer. "There just ain't, Jas, and right now I'm not goin' to question that. In the shape we're in right now — there better not be."

Jasper began to look back more often, frowning as he did so. It was the only real concern he had, except for the condition of their Rafter W horses, and those two things dove-tailed in his mind. If a posse showed up, there was now no way under the wet skies they could out-run it, and if it was big enough there was no way for them to fight clear of it either.

John saw his partner's expression. "Quit worrying. It ain't back there and that's what matters."

They saw a ranch. A set of log buildings to the west over closer to the coachroad, in fact about the same distance westward as that squatter's cabin had been. There was a big old prosperous-looking log barn with a network of working-corrals, and a number of outbuildings as well as a low, rambling main-house.

"Now that," exclaimed John Hall, "is the answer to a man's prayer."

131

There was one small stand of trees, southward, so they had to walk another mile then turn and make their approach from the south.

Thin smoke rose from the main-house, in what Jasper assumed was the kitchen because it was at the rear of the building, and a second thin tailing of smoke rose above a bunkhouse which was between the main-house and the big log barn, on the west side of the yard.

"Horses," John said, from in among the trees, pointing. "Ten or twelve head in that farthest corral."

Jasper shook water from his hat then leaned to look harder. He smiled, spat amber, re-set his hat and let go a big sigh. The walking these past few miles through gumbo mud had taken a lot out of him. He had never thought of himself as old, and only lately had he even conceded to himself that he might be ageing. What had brought that to his attention was the feet which swelled for no apparent reason, and the need he'd been developing lately for more sleep.

But right now, water running off his long black slicker in rivulets, his stooped body inside without a shred of resilience left in the knees and ankles, and his tiredness solid enough to interfere with his thinking processes, he said something he probably would never have otherwise said, "This here is my last long ride. I figured it would be, when I got to thinkin' we'd ought to make one big raid then quit."

John was squinting ahead and acted as though he had not heard. Finally he turned to tie the bay horse and turn back. "Look yonder. We can sneak from these trees along the rear of the house, behind the bunkhouse and get all the way to that far corral without bein' exposed more'n a couple of little places." He turned. "Well. Tie the damned animal, Jas, and let's get goin'. We can't just set down and wait for nightfall you know."

Jasper turned and obediently tied his horse.

11
A Change Of Horses

The drizzle had not let up since it had begun. Neither had it increased in intensity. There was no wind, no particular cold, just a steady, chilling drizzle in a kind of damp warmth which people, for all their protective innovations such as raincoats, could not escape.

Jasper could close the little metal fasteners on his slicker now that he had shed most of his loot, but all that did was keep body-heat inside, so while the chill worked through, he also perspired a little.

He would have given one hundred dollars, gold, for a drink of strong whisky. Instead, he studied the area on ahead and when John started ahead, he followed.

There were three windows in the back of the main-house, but there were none in the back-wall of the log bunkhouse, although there was a door and the same kind of little porch with an overhang that had also been built on the front.

They could not guess how many people were inside the main-house, and except that they could make educated guesses having worked for outfits this size years back, they would have been unable to guess about the men at the bunkhouse, but as Jasper saw it, it would make no difference if there were four or five riders in there, or just one or two, if they got caught stealing horses the punishment would be the same.

But he had no intention of being caught, so when John paused before crossing the muddy ground between main-house and bunkhouse, Jasper said, "Walk. Keep your hand on your gun and don't try to run for it — just walk."

Men made noises, or they slipped, running under these circumstances. They also attracted attention, which, if someone happened to be looking out, might arouse a suspicion. Men with their backs to the main-house walking to the rear of the bunkhouse would look like any other men.

John obeyed but he did it with an obvious effort. He was leaning as though to bolt, right up until they got to the rear of the bunkhouse, then relaxed a little because now they could not be seen from the main-house.

The big old barn was dry with a soft humming sound made by light rainfall upon the high roof. Jasper stepped inside for a moment, to shake water off his old hat, to kick mud from his boots, and to just stand where it was dry for a little while.

John was impatient. He'd look out the rear barn-opening, pull back, then look again. It irritated the older man but he said nothing.

They they borrowed a pair of lass ropes from saddles astraddle the pole and went out again, northwards to the corrals.

The smartest horses had crowded up alongside the barn's northwall where two-foot overhanging log eaves protected them from direct rainfall. The others were sniffling the ground for the last few untrampled stalks of hay from their early-morning feeding.

John hovered briefly, decided on a *grulla* gelding under the eaves, and slid through the stringers, rope in hand. All the horses became alert now, and John remained outside, looking in the direction of the bunkhouse. He could not see the main-house, the barn cut it off, but he felt no particular trepidation. Unless they stirred up the horses or made a lot of noise, on a day like this no one was going to be ambling around outside.

The *grulla* had to be cornered or roped and John had enough presence of mind not to rope him. That would have started a lot of rushing and running. It never took much to excite horses accustomed to being roped, all a man had to do was shake out his loop and make a couple of overhead swings with it. There was a better way of playing out the loop to one side, guessing the distance and the direction the horse would jump, then make a backhand overhead pass bringing the big loop down for the horse to run into it, but you could only get away with that once; afterwards the horses were thoroughly spooked and savvy.

John swore and got red in the face because the *grulla* was wise to all the moves in this game. He knew John would try to head him, keep him away from the other horses, and tried to sidle past by hugging the east side of the corral. John had to jump through thick mud to head him. Then the *grulla* stood deceptively head-hung, but this time *he* was anticipated. John did not approach from the front, which he was supposed to do, he came in on an angle which cut the horse off from swinging back or rushing past.

The *grulla* submitted meekly once he understood there was nothing else to do.

John cursed him, yanked the rope tight and led him to the gate which Jasper was holding half open. As Jas took the rope he said, "Leave that grey be. Folks can see a horse like that on a day like this for five miles."

It was true, but not only on gloomy days. If there was one colour horse outlaws avoided it was a light grey — what most people called a 'white' horse.

John did not comment as he turned back with the second lass rope, looking angry or disgusted, perhaps a little of both. He made the selection while moving, and this time the horse, having seen what had happened to the *grulla* and knowing from experience that inside a corral there was no way to escape, simply stood and waited. John caught him and led this one out too.

A little gust of cold wind arrived, travelling low along the soggy earth. It fled southeastward and there was no other gust in its wake.

Jasper had squeezed water from his gloves, and afterwards had a hard time getting them back on again. Wet buckskin did not pull worth a darn. He looked their new mounts over, bobbed his head just once, and stepped slightly away from the barn's rear wall until he could see the bunkhouse. The smoke was still rising and that was all. He jerked his head as a signal for John to lead off. They could have climbed up bareback but Jasper did not have enough spring left, and they were both still somewhat weighted with a segment of their treasure.

Jasper might have gone back to the trees where his horse was tethered, in a different way, but John trudged past, still sullenly upset over the way the *grulla* had forced a delay. Jasper shrugged and also went back behind the bunkhouse, across the open area to the northwest corner of the main-house, and beyond. When they halted out back of the large ranch-owner's residence nothing had changed. The stovepipe was still trailing a thin spiral of grey smoke, the drizzle was just as monotonously falling as ever, onward was the open area and beyond it the trees where their horses waited.

Jasper had an intuitive feeling, one of those things which did not submit to rational analysis. Nor was he the kind of man who heeded them very often. He'd had dozens of them in years past, and blessed few had ever amounted to a damn.

Up ahead John did not even look back, he simply tugged his horse and started hiking, head low in the face of the rainfall.

He got all the way across to the trees. Jasper was still a few yards from the trees, avoiding his partner's tracks. It was better to slither and stick in fresh mud than it was to do worse using someone else's imprints.

One of the tired onward horses nickered softly. John fiercely cursed it and when he got up there, without knowing which horse had done that, he kicked the handsome bay in the stomach as hard as he could swing a leg.

Jasper had seen these temper-tantrums before. He had also seen sullen moods in his partner, but neither of them occurred often enough to bother Jasper, and perhaps today John was entitled to feel this way. It had been an ordeal right from the moment last night when that old man had tried to shoot them from the rear door of the general store. There had been no real disasters, just a series of nagging little worrisome things like that horse nickering. It had not actually made enough noise to be heard inside a log house, but it was something else which could have created difficulties. It hadn't, and in fact Jasper was satisfied that it wouldn't, but it *could* have. Maybe that was not important in other trades, but in Jasper's trade it was very important. Every hazard was very important to men in Jasper's trade because they were not allowed to be mistaken very often. Usually, in fact, they were allowed no mistakes at all.

This was the second pair of horses they had set free with pressed-flat saddle-marks on their backs, with rubbed places where the cheek-pieces of bridles had snugly set. But this time the abandoned horses seemed content to stand exactly where they had been released, head-hung and water dripping.

John yanked his fresh horse left, then right, and the animal understood at once: This was not a man to fight back at.

Jasper had already made his judgment of the *grulla.* He was not a young horse and he was wise in all the ways required to care for himself, to do what was demanded of him with the least expenditure of energy and without going over the limit of what he could get away with before someone rawhided him. He was a ridgling but Jasper did not know it. Neither had John known it. John could be forgiven but Jasper had been around an awful lot of horses; he should have known, except that back yonder outside the corral he was not the least bit interested in the sex of those horses, just in the ability of one of them to carry him safely on southward.

John stood a moment beside his fresh horse, which was fully rigged out. He gazed back at those two buildings where smoke was rising. Then he turned and hauled himself astride, waited for Jasper to come on, then he said, "Lucky bastards are settin' inside the bunkhouse playin' poker and drinking coffee with the store poppin' at their backs."

Jasper did not have to look back, he knew what was going on at the bunkhouse. He also knew something else. "Yeah — and they'll earn twelve dollars this month, and next month, and when we're settin' beside a train window warm and comfortable, leavin' this gawddamn territory, they'll still be ridin' in the heat, cussin' the snowdrifts, riskin' their stupid heads — and gettin' twelve a month and found."

The fresh horses made a difference, but Jasper cautioned his partner; this pair might have to last a long while.

They rode six or seven miles closer to the hills, to the low, thick mountains beyond the foothills, and came upon a line-shack which they scouted-up first, then tied up and entered.

Riders had been there not too long before. Best of all, two pack-boxes nailed to a wall near a small iron stove were full of tinned food.

John said, "I don't give a damn, Jas, we've

earned the right to dry out and eat."

Jasper went to take the horses out back, and tied them under the shed-roof back there, out of sight. John built a fire, selecting only dry wood, and when Jasper returned he was frying tinned venison with onions and was making a pot of coffee which was the most wonderfull smell Jasper could remember ever having smelled before, even though he had smelled it just about every day of his life for the past forty years.

Steam rose from their slickers. When the room was warm they shed them. John even shed his hat and Jasper hung soggy gloves to dry out.

"How far we come, you reckon?" the younger man asked. "By gawd, it seems like a hunnert damned miles to me."

"Not even quite half that," Jasper replied, and at the look he got Jas shrugged stooped shoulders. "This here valley ain't that wide by half, John, and we're just now gettin' to the foothills."

John let that pass and turned to the next most interesting thing to him. "Where the hell is the pursuit?"

That, as a matter of fact, had been coming to increasingly trouble Jasper. He had no idea where it was, but he knew for a fact it had to be out there, somewhere. No town

143

the size of Cutler was going to let a little rainfall and mud deter it from going in pursuit of outlaws who had raided the town.

"Maybe went the wrong way," suggested Jasper, "or maybe they come onto a couple other riders and hauled them in instead of us." For the look of scepticism he got Jasper threw up his hands. "Damned if I know, John. All I can tell you is that I'm darned glad they didn't come up on us while we was ridin' them rode-down Rafter W horses."

They ate, drank coffee, sat loose at the old table allowing stove-heat to soak through into muscles and nerves. John rolled a smoke from tobacco he found in the line-shack. Jasper had a fresh chew, his first one since last night. He even smiled a little, tiredly it was true, but with a full feeling as he scratched then dropped the hat back down.

"I'm not goin' to do a lick of work again, maybe for the rest of my life. It's been hardship after hardship since I was a button; sweat and melt and freeze and be afraid and get hopes that never came true, and more hardship." He continued to smile. "Not from this day on, John. From the time we find the train-cars, get some new clothes and head out, I'm never goin' to ride at night again, nor in the rain, nor go hungry — nor any of the rest of it."

John laughed, reached for his cup of coffee, and one of the horses out back under the overhang nickered. John's hand and arm froze in mid-air. He stared at Jasper. The older man briefly stared back, then arose without a sound, palming his Colt as he stood up.

John did not move from the table, but he picked up the sawed-off shotgun and swung it two-handedly in the direction of the door.

12
THE LINE SHACK

The drizzle had stopped, which was the first thing Jasper noticed. They had been riding in it since it had started during the darkness and it had been continuing for so long its abrupt absence made Jasper waste a second glancing at the leaden sky.

There was no reason to believe more rainfall would not come. The sky was just as lowering and dark and swollen-looking as it had been during the rainfall. Visibility was not particularly good either, despite a cessation in the light downpour. But it was good enough.

There was a string of riders dead ahead in front of the line-shack, sitting their horses, hands in plain sight, slickers shiny and hats still dripping a little. One man Jasper recognised at once. He had a carbine balancing across his lap. The town marshal from Cutler. The other men became a blur as Jasper's breath stopped in his throat while he and the string of horsemen gazed back and forth.

They simply sat there, eight of them on horses with muddy shanks, armed with Winchesters and sixguns. Jasper had his Colt dangling at his side. The lawman said, "Toss that gun out here." He did not snarl it nor make it sound like a command, but it definitely was one.

None of them had guns showing. Jasper could jump back and slam the door and roll sideways before any of them drew and fired. He was sure he could accomplish it and re-gripped the gun at his side.

As though capable of mind-reading Town Marshal Craig Stanton spoke again. "Mister, there are four men around back looking at those horses you fellers — borrowed. They ride for the outfit where you got those horses. And mister, Rafter W's on the way, coming south on the stageroad. . . . Now toss the gun out."

Behind Jasper, John was on his feet, the scattergun gripped. He had belatedly heard that voice out front, had only looked around his partner's shoulder though, as some of the words began to reach him and make sense.

He pulled the door wider and jumped past, swinging the sawed-off scattergun. It was a mistake. Someone shot him from the east side of the front wall and he struggled to hold balance, tugging at both triggers of his shotgun, another man shot him from the west corner of the front wall. John slid along the wall, then dropped the scattergun and turned loose all over.

No one said a word for a while, then Marshal Stanton spoke again to Jasper in that same calm, almost gentle tone. "It wasn't loaded. The storekeeper told me this morning he had been afraid old Frank might use the damned thing sometime, one of those moments when old Frank'd get all upset by a loud noise maybe, so he unloaded it. That scattergun hasn't had charges in it for five, six years. . . . Mister; pitch out the handgun. This is the last time. Pitch it out."

Jasper obeyed, tossed the gun into the mud and avoided glancing to his left where John was lying.

Two men approached from each end of the shack; four of them with guns. One of them, a red-headed man with very dark green eyes, reached with a strong arm and shoved Jasper along the wall, then watched while another cowboy made a complete search and flung Jasper's bootknife out into the mud near the sixgun.

The possemen dismounted and sought

148

places to tie up. They did not pay the least bit of attention to the dead man, except that one of them scooped up the harmless scattergun saying Cal Hotchkiss back at town would want it back.

This man had to step over John to reach that gun. He did it as though John were just a small impediment, without once looking down, but the town marshal came forward, gazed a moment at ashen Jasper White, then went over and flopped John face up. Two of those little buckskin pouches had broken a bone shirtfront-button. Craig picked them up, read names, shoved them into a jacket pocket and shook his head.

He turned, facing Jasper. "You got 'em inside your shirt too." It was a statement, not a question, but Jasper nodded anyway. "If you fellers knew that shotgun warn't loaded, you didn't have to shoot him," he told the lawman.

One of the rough ranch-hands answered that. "Ten minutes after you thievin' bastards stole our horses, them horses you left behind went over to the corrals and set to squealin' with the horses inside the corral." He smiled a little. "We was on your trail then minutes later . . . Mister, that partner of yours was goin' to die anyway, and we had no way of knowin' he hadn't maybe

discovered he was carryin' an empty scattergun, and maybe picked up some loads
for it . . . But he was goin' to die anyway . . .
horse stealin' . . . that's the penalty for it."

Craig Stanton did not interrupt the cowboy but he did not seem greatly impressed
by the rangeman's statement either. "Put
the rest of the pouches from inside your
shirt into your hat," he told Jasper.

Three possemen ploughed past to enter
the line-shack. One of them found the
uneaten meal and wolfed it down. The other
two had coffee.

Jasper had an ace in the hole, but until he
was satisfied it was safe to use it he simply
did what he was told to do, and did nothing
to upset the rangemen or the possemen. But
when the newness of the shootout and
capture had worn off, the possemen went
around back to look at the pair of stolen
horses, or went inside to eat, Jasper called
Craig Stanton over.

They were along the front wall when he
said, "Marshal, them is just a small part of
the sacks out of that safe. Just a small part."

Craig nodded his head and their eyes did
not waver from one another. "I know that."

"Well, Marshal, I know where a hell of a
lot of them little sacks is buried, and hidden

where no one could find it in a hunnert years."

"Do you for a fact?"

"Yes sir; and I'm going to make a trade with you. Get all them boys inside and leave a horse untied out here — and that's all. I'll give you a drawin' right now where that cache is."

Craig stoically considered Jasper for a while, then turned, sloshed out to his horse, lifted a pocket-flap from behind and below the cantle, pulled forth something and held it up. Four sacks with names on them, also with mud on them. He dropped them back, buckled the saddle-bag and trudged back, all without saying a word.

Jasper's colour was bad. The lawman said, "There went your last chance, mister. By the way, there wasn't one cache, there was two of them. . . . It was like shootin' fish in a rainbarrel. We followed tracks all the way, to both caches, over where you fellers stole the horses, then on down here."

Jasper said, "We never saw you. We kept a watch but we never saw you even once."

"We came south on the stageroad. Better footin' over there." Craig studied the dirty, unkempt appearance of Jasper. "Had two scouts out east and west of the road. The fellers shaggin' you boys stayed far back.

Better'n a mile back. The rest of us kept in touch with them and hurried southward on the road." Craig reached to pull out his makings and start rolling a smoke. "Which one are you — Hall or White?"

"White. Jasper White."

"Care to roll one?"

"No thanks, I chew."

"That darned fool carried that scattergun all this while and never once broke it to see if it was loaded?"

Jasper shrugged. He had not paid much attention to the sawed off shotgun, but if it were known, he too had assumed the thing was loaded.

The lawman said, "That old feller back at the counter — old man with sleeve-socks . . . ?"

"Yeah. What of him?"

"Which one of you shot back at him?"

"Why?"

"You hit him, Jasper. He's dead."

"Well, Christ, he was a hunnert years old."

Craig turned as that red-headed range-man came out of the shack with a tin cup of black coffee and offered it to the lawman. As he did this he said, "Marshal, it's a hell of a long ride back and we got plenty of bunks at the ranch. . . . You could light out first thing in the morning." The red-head turned a lethal gaze at Jasper White. "You boys can bed down and we'll chain this son of a bitch in the root-cellar for you."

Jasper knew without another word being spoken what this cowman had in mind: Take Jasper out in the wee hours when everyone was asleep — and hang him. Gag him, bind his ankles and elbows, and hang him.

He would have protested but Marshal Stanton spoke first. "I'm sure obliged. That's a real decent offer and if I didn't have to be back in Cutler come morning, by golly I'd sure take you up on it." Stanton reached to slap the cowman affably on the back.

As the red-headed cowman trudged back inside Jasper said, "*You* might ride out in the morning, Marshal, but *I* never would."

Craig sampled the coffee then offered the cup as he said, "Mister White, I didn't come down in that last rain. You care for some coffee?"

Jasper shook his head. He'd had coffee a half hour back when he and John had been sitting in there, drying and relaxed and replete. How in the hell could everything under the sun change so quickly? He glanced over where his partner was lying, his face beginning to assume the same ashen, dull grey shade as the threatening

153

sky, except that John had a faint tinge of green too, which the sky entirely lacked.

Craig caught the direction of his prisoner's gaze and spoke. "I guess I could have told them the shotgun was not loaded."

Jasper brought his attention back, and waited. Craig smiled a little, scarcely wasted a glance at the corpse, then spoke again.

"I been in this business quite a few years, Mister White. Horse-stealin' — well, you can usually fetch them to the jailhouse — and some of the other things you boys did last night — even murder, sometimes, but there's one thing folks just can't abide, and that's to believe outlaws are going to escape. The men with me been gettin' soaked and hungry and tired and frazzled-out, afraid you boys was going to get away. And those rangemen in there — same thing. Mister White, I know how folks react. I could no more have defied the whole batch of men than I could have brought both you boys back for trial."

Jasper listened, and stared. "You mean you deliberately didn't tell them that scattergun was not loaded?"

"Yup. Isn't that a hell of a thing to do? Except that now I think I'll be able to get back to town with you alive." Craig showed a hint of smile at the outer corners of his mouth.

The other men came back out, their mood improved at least to the extent that as they moved off to get their horses they joked a little back and forth.

Craig Stanton accepted this as the best omen so far and when the red-headed cowman returned with those two horses stolen from his corrals, saddled and ready, he handed one set of reins to Craig and led the other horse over, and as business-like as though he required help pitching a buck deer across a horse he said, "Couple you fellers lend me a hand, this feller's limp as a rag."

Craig pointed and Jasper stepped over to mount the same horse he had ridden before his capture. Craig found his own animal and rode back to sit beside his prisoner. "Let me tell you something, Mister White — Rafter W is up the road somewhere. That's the outfit you stole those first two horses from. The feller who owns the outfit probably wouldn't lynch you, but he's got three riders who'd kill you on sight if they dared, so I'm giving you this advice hopin' you'll follow it — don't get five feet from my side and don't do a darn thing anyone can afterwards say they figured you was going for a hide-out gun over. Understand?"

Jasper had been thinking of the long ride back. He was bone-tired as it was, getting down this far. The thought of making the full ride back made him rummage deep down for a reserve of strength which over the years had always been there. Today, it was not there. He nodded dumbly as the riders turned over in the direction of the stageroad. Jasper shivered inside his slicker but it was not cold, he was dry and full of food, nor was it raining again although it seemed about to start any moment.

The men scarcely heeded him on the ride back up the road in the general direction of that ranch he and John had raided during the rainfall. Those cowboys evidently took their cue from the red-headed cowman, and he seemed less inclined now to talk of hang-ropes than he had been earlier, when he and his riders had met the possemen and joined them. Craig was right; that one killing had satisfied them.

Jasper got a chew and rode with both hands atop the saddlehorn until they reached the place where the rangemen would turn off following ruts inland, then Jasper expected the red-headed cowman to demand his horse. He didn't, he eyed Jasper with almost casual contempt and said,

"I'll be up to town the next couple days, Marshal. Corral 'em and I'll pick 'em up on my way home again." He looked again at Jasper. "You old son of a bitch," he said, and reined away leading his riders westerly in an easy lope.

The road was grey and arrow-straight for more miles than they could see as they resumed the ride. One of the possemen, a man who was vaguely familiar to Jasper, said, "You figure to just keep goin', Craig? The only decent dry place to put up for the night between here and town is some squatter's shack about six, eight miles dead ahead and to the right of the road."

Jasper remembered that place. Corrals there had had no horses. Craig's answer was revealing. "I think we'd ought to just keep going as long as we can." A man groaned and Craig looked over at him. "Just in case those fellers back there change their minds," he said, without explaining what they might change their minds about. The others understood and so did Jasper, riding beside the big, thick-shouldered lawman. He spat aside and fixed his gaze far ahead.

He had lost his final gamble. All the other raids he'd carried off successfully had kept him supplied with enough money, but this was the last toss of the dice, and by gawd it had come up snake-eyes.

Maybe John had come off best after all. He sure as hell hadn't had long to reflect upon what this failure meant. Jasper spat again and gazed at the lawman beside him. He was not just big and solid, but now for the first time that easy-going, affable expression he wore meant something different to Jasper. Maybe he was lazy; maybe he was just savvy at his trade and did not have to work himself down to a nubbin to succeed at it.

He had allowed a murder to be committed right before his own gawddamned eyes, and had not changed expression; still looked affable and easy-going when he had seen John go down holding that useless damned scattergun.

In every trade there were extenuating circumstances, and Jasper knew it very well because his own trade was actually built on them, but this was the first time in all his brushes with the law, he had ever encountered one of those mitigations on the side of the law.

He said, "Murder, Marshal; plain and simple murder back there."

Craig rode a yard before speaking. "I guess it was, Mister White. If he hadn't jumped out there, though . . ."

"But you knew he'd die, Marshal."

"Yeah, that's true, but I already explained that to you. If I figured to get back with one of you alive I was goin' to have to keep my ace in the hole — the shotgun."

Craig looked at the sullen dark sky. "We're goin' to get rained on some more, Mister White. By the way — how are you holding up?"

Jasper said no more. He rode slouched and hunched, chewed and occasionally spat, listened to the desultory talk behind him, and remembered John's alternating periods of bubbling exuberance and sullen weariness.

They had been partners, had worked expertly as a rustling team, never quarrelled and. . . . "Hell," he said hopelessly, straightened a little in the saddle, and kept on riding.

When the first sprinkles came he tugged his hat low so water would run off the front of it, snapped the old slicker to the gullet and did not say another word.

13
END OF THE TRAIL

They were two-thirds of the way to Cutler before a small crew of riders approached them from the east, over where they had evidently been following a wide, muddy trail, easy enough to follow since the posse-men had passed down the original sign made by Jasper and John Hall.

Jeff Wayman sat gazing at the surviving outlaw. His men including the *vaquero* named Sanchez, gazed from the corpse flopping along belly-down in the rain, to Jasper, their faces uncompromising and hard-set while Craig Stanton explained all that happened.

Jasper's tired body was shrunken inside his black slicker, his unshaven, dirty face with its dull eyes, looked out upon the newcomers with an expression of fatalistic disregard.

Only when Rafter W's rangeboss said, "What'n hell did you bring him alive for?"

did Jasper show any interest. The town marshal passed that off in his deep, calm voice by saying, "You fellers want to ride back with us?" It was his way of saying he would not listen to war-talk, evidently, and Rafter W must have interpreted it that way because nothing more was said which would have been threatening.

They had to ride north anyway, so they joined the posse. Jasper had no illusions. Maybe the lawman had satisfied that red-headed cowman back yonder and his lynch-rope riders, but this was a different set of men. No one had satisfied them, nor was it possible for Marshal Stanton to do it, unless he was willing to let them take his prisoner, and that seemed very unlikely. In fact, as they moseyed on up the roadway he leaned and quietly reiterated the warning he had given Jasper earlier.

"Ride close and don't do anything foolish."

Jasper could not have done anything "foolish." He did not even have his bootknife, let alone his sixgun, and the horse he was riding could not have out-run those Rafter W animals; the best in Long Grass Valley.

A couple of miles farther along Cal Hamilton eased up beside Jasper and turned a craggy, hostile face with rainwater dripping from his old hat. "You're a lucky son of a bitch," he said. "We wanted to run you fellers down first."

Jasper understood the look and turned to gaze on up the roadway. He had gone through a number of emotions since first looking out the doorway of that line-shack. He was worn out from within. The fear of being lynched did not bother him very much now. It had earlier; had kept him riding in fear for miles, but too much had been taken out of him over the past twenty or so hours. He eventually looked over at the rangeboss and said, "Too bad you didn't," and when Hamilton faintly scowled, Jasper turned away again.

They did not reach Cutler until late, in the silken darkness when the town was abed. There was still a light up at the saloon, and two lamp-posts, one at either end of the wide roadway, marked the limits of Cutler with enclosed lamps. Otherwise, excluding a pair of buggy lamps on each side of the liverybarn's front doorway, Cutler was sleeping, which was about right, for although the drizzle had ceased while the crowd of horsemen had been a couple of miles down the south coachroad, everything was still wet, and water dripped from eaves. No one would be abroad on a night like this — except outlaws and lawmen.

The nighthawk knew Jasper by sight and looked woodenly as Craig Stanton helped the outlaw down. They led the other stolen horse out back somewhere. That was the last Jasper ever saw of his partner.

He sat on a hardwood wall-bench, old slicker shiny and beaded with adobe mud at the bottom.

A posseman came over, dropped down, blew out a big breath, thumbed back his water-heavy hat and fished forth a pony of whisky. "Take a couple of swallers," he told Jasper.

The whisky burned like fire but afterwards its benign glow helped immeasurably. The posseman took back his bottle, took several swallows himself then walked over to care for his horse without looking back.

Craig got Jeff Wayman to help him carry the heavy saddlebags to the jailhouse office. Sanchez and Caloway Hamilton followed but at the door Craig shook his head so they remained outside, murmuring grimly to each other.

Inside, Jeff and the lawman dumped all those muddy little pouches into a lower desk drawer with Jasper sitting over near the gun-rack with its chain through six trigger-guards, watching.

When that was taken care of the lawman shed his slicker, tossed aside his wet hat, shucked his gloves and scratched his middle while gazing at the captive. Jeff Wayman was younger and fresher. At least he acted fresher, although he must have also been in the saddle many hours.

He asked Jasper where he and John Hall were from. Jasper gestured indifferently. "A lot of places. It don't matter."

Craig was rummaging in some crates behind his desk when the horse rancher said, "How come you to raid my place — did you come down from the north, and come up to the bluff above my range?"

Jasper nodded. "We camped atop the bluff." He saw the lawman straightening up with two posters in his hands. He did not have to see them, so he looked at the horse-rancher. "You'll get your horses back. We left them down near a cow outfit a few miles from where the posse caught us." He shook his head, it still bothered him that the posse had out-smarted him so well.

Craig handed the dodgers to Wayman and while the younger man was looking at them the town marshal picked up a ring of brass keys.

So far he had offered no admonitions, had not done as most lawmen would have done, commented about the evils of a life of crime and so forth. Maybe he was too tired to give a damn; Jasper surely was as he dragged up to his feet ready to be locked in. They exchanged a look then Craig went over and pushed back the cell-room door. Without a word between them he herded Jasper down into the clammy cell-room, locked him into a cell and as he paused he said, "The circuit-riding judge shows up in Cutler twice a month. It'll be a few days before he'll be here for your hearing. You can think about your defence. If you got one."

Back up front Jeff Wayman was standing at the window when Craig returned. He had rolled and lit a smoke. "It would have been better if they'd both got killed," he said matter-of-factly. "Folks aren't going to like being robbed nor having that old man killed, Craig."

The lawman tossed aside his key-ring. That statement had sounded like a warning so he smiled at the horse-rancher. "We got back the money. Like he told you, you'll get back your horses."

"And the old man?"

"Well; that's why we got judges, Jeff."

Wayman gently shook his head. "And ropes," he muttered.

Craig retained his smile. "Not as long as

he's my prisoner, Jeff. I've never had to shotgun a lynch-mob but I could if I had to." Craig stood gazing at the younger man. "Go home, get some rest, and I appreciate you fellers helping . . . Jeff, let the law handle it."

Wayman picked up his hat. "Sure. *I* will. But there's going to be folks around town who won't want to." He went to the door and turned one more time, hand lying upon the latch. "Any danger of another pair coming along tonight?" He nodded toward the drawer where they had put those pouches and small bales of greenbacks.

Craig's smile lingered. "They'll get a hell of a surprise if they do."

After the rancher had departed Craig swore under his breath. He was not worried about more robbers, but to be sure he was going to have to sit here until morning when Hotchkiss's store was open so he could take the money back to the safe, and what he had looked forward to on the ride back had been a nice warm bed and a long night of sleep.

He made coffee, drank one cup, then filled two more cups and went down into the cell-room to offer one to the stooped, depressed man in the cell. He had no other prisoners, had not had any others for a couple of months.

Jasper came to the front of the cell, wordlessly accepted the cup and tasted its contents. "Bitter as hell," he said.

Craig nodded agreeably. "Some things I'm good at. Makin' decent coffee isn't one of them."

"But you do pretty well at posse-riding."

Craig leaned on the straps of rolled steel. "Well; stands to reason you boys would be watching your back-trail like hawks. . . . Mister White, I've done this before, a lot of times."

Jasper believed it. He had been sitting there in the feeble light of one lamp hanging out in the corridor thinking of how carefully he had planned, how careful he had been and how it had seemed everything was favourable — and how it had all come unravelled in a matter of minutes. He had also thought of something else.

"That old man . . . Hell; he was shakin' like a leaf. His eyes was waterin' and all. . . . And maybe you won't believe this, but he fired first."

"Yeah, I believe it," stated the lawman. "I examined the gun he used. Thing is, *he* was right and *you* were wrong. The law of self-defence don't work under those circumstances, Mister White."

"Is there lynch-talk?"

Craig nodded. "Some."

They looked steadily at one another through an interval of silence before Jasper also said, "And you . . . You let 'em have John."

Craig offered no rebuttal to this. "It's different when you are my prisoner. I might as well hang it up if I ever let lynchers take a prisoner out of here."

Jasper drained the cup and handed it out through the bars. "How'll I come out of this?" he asked.

"Alive," stated the marshal. "And with maybe a life sentence in prison for murder. How old are you?"

"It don't matter."

Craig agreed. "I guess it don't at that. A life sentence sometimes means you can come up for a parole hearing in about ten or fifteen years, on a murder charge, and providin' the folks down here don't protest it. But I reckon you're right, Mister White, at your age it don't matter."

"Marshal . . . ?"

"Yeah."

"I got some kinfolk back east."

Craig stood waiting for the rest of it.

"A son about twenty-five years old by now. Well; I haven't heard of him in — since he was real little. After we got settled in the west we was to send back for him. He was too little to stand the crossing."

"And a wife?"

Jasper said, "She died." He looked around then back out at the lawman. "I'd as leave the boy never found out about me."

Craig could understand this but there was nothing he could do about it so he said, "We don't have a newspaper in Cutler — but there'll be other newspapers I expect, once they sentence you."

Jasper continued to study the calm, broad face through the bars out in the little corridor, then he turned away saying, "Good night, Marshal."

Craig walked back to the office with the pair of empty cups, sluiced them in a bucket behind the stove and re-hung them from pegs behind the stove. He yawned, barred the cell-room door, stoked the stove, locked the roadside door from inside the office, went to the desk to kick out of his boots, which were heavy with mud and water, turned down the lamp and leaned back in his desk-chair with his sixgun atop the desk within quick reach.

He expected no trouble. No one could get inside without giving him plenty of notice of their intention. He thought about the stooped old outlaw and shook his head about a man still being in that business when he was Jasper's age. Usually, if they survived at all, they did not get themselves killed or hanged or imprisoned, they quit long before.

But this one had been successful a long while. Too long a while in fact. The rewards on both of them, White and Hall, would more than defray the burial of all three of them — the old man and the pair of outlaws. What was left over would go into what the Town Council called its "undistributed reserve," which was another way of saying it went to support the school and to pay the town marshal's wages.

He arose and went to look out the front window. The sky was as clear as a bell with stars showing in a high, clean-washed vault of heaven. The rain was gone and with it all the overhead vestiges of it.

He went back to his chair, hoisted both heavy legs atop the littered old desk and closed his eyes. He was asleep within moments and did not hear a thing, not even the little rustling sounds down in his cellroom. He was a large man who required considerable food and lots of sleep, even when he wasn't as worn-down as he had been when he'd got back to town tonight.

The stove kept his office warm until shortly before dawn even though that glass-clear sky brought a return of a strong cold front. He did not open his eyes nor move in the chair until seeping cold made him conscious of the pre-dawn chill and he opened his eyes, saw fishbelly grey light filtering in, coughed, stood up and went over in his stocking-feet to shove a couple more sticks of wood in the stove.

Then he went over to the front window to look up and down the silent, grey and empty roadway before setting down to tug on his boots.

The light steadily brightened, but slowly, but there was no sun and would not be any for several hours yet. He went out back to wash in the alleyway at the rack, and to shave in poor light, then returned to the office, leathered his gun and heaved a big sigh as he groped among the desk-litter for his keys and went over to open the cell-room door. Cold air came out.

Old White must have shivered a little last night.

He walked down, reached to turn up the wick of the hanging corridor lamp, and saw the utterly still form dangling at the end of a rope of blankets, boots off, hat on the

floor, puffy face as grey as the newday weak
light.

14
A STRANGER

It was a shock, of course. In law-enforcement work people saw considerable death and violence but not very many suicides inside jail cells where blankets had been fashioned into a hang-rope.

He took White down and placed him upon the bunk then checked an urge to swear, not out of any deference for the dead but a few memories returned now to make him gaze at the dead man. The way Jasper had said, "Good night, Marshal," and the way he had phlegmatically agreed when Craig had said it did not matter how old he was. And there was the nagging shame which would have been responsible for old Jasper not wanting his kinfolk to know, especially the son he had last seen as an infant.

There were probably other reasons about which Craig could only guess. Anyway, now he had to get Turgeson the carpenter to make up a box, and he had to get the preacher ready, the grave-diggers, the under-taker — who also ran a small furniture business — and he had to prepare a note for the circuit-riding judge to explain why there would be no need for a trial.

As for the town, by nine o'clock after Craig had notified the preacher — whose tongue had a hinge in the middle so that it would wag at both ends — the carpenter and several other people, word spread from north to south in minutes. Cal Hotchkiss came over acting spiteful, now that he knew the money had been recovered and that, finally, both of the outlaws were dead.

"You should have supplied a decent rope," he told Craig. "Just in case them blankets broke, and where is the money, Craig? I'd like to get it back in the safe. Folks could get their faith shaken in my bank. . . . You kept it there, in just a plain desk drawer all night, for heaven's sake?"

Craig was annoyed. "It's still here, isn't it?"

"But just a desk-drawer . . . !" Hotchkiss threw up his hands.

Craig began loading the storekeeper's arms, kept loading them until Caleb Hotchkiss squawked a protest, then Craig turned to hold the door for him and to smile into his upturned, straining face. "I'll stand here,

Cal, and protect you from outlaws on the way across the road, and think how it'll boost folks' confidence in your bank, seein' you staggerin' back to the store with all their savings."

He gave the storekeeper a little shove, and as Hotchkiss gasped and went unsteadily toward the centre of the road Craig went back to the drawer to shove bales of greenbacks into his shirt-front to leave his hands free to carry the balance of those small pouches.

When he got outside people were standing here and there on both sides of the roadway, some in small groups gawking and hurriedly talking, others stoically watching with nothing to say, as the recovered wealth of Long Grass Valley was carried back to the general store.

Old Frank was missing from his high old clerk's stool back in the dingy rear of the store, otherwise nothing looked different. The mess had been cleaned up, the scattered papers and ledgers put back. That gun which had been kept inside the safe was missing. Craig still had it across the road, but in time it would also return. Just old Frank would never come back.

Caleb was leaning on his desk breathing hard. He looked accusingly upwards as

Craig Stanton shoved his way in to toss down his light load and pull out the bales of greenbacks. He waited until Hotchkiss had caught his breath and went to bend low at the safe-front. "Suppose," said the storekeeper, "a few of those sacks or bundles are missing?"

Craig studied the long, bony back of the leaning older man, irritation rising. "Why then, Cal, since you're the banker and all, you'll just have to make them good."

Hotchkiss straightened around as though he had been stung. "Me? *You're* the law hereabouts, Craig!"

"You sure don't expect *me* to make it good. I did my share by finding those fellers and fetching them back. And now I'll do the rest of it by buryin' them." He smiled and tapped the storekeeper on the chest. "You're the feller's been talking folks into saving in your store — put it where it'll be safe — Cal, I've heard you say that a hundred times."

Craig left, passed up through the store and went out front. He had not counted the little pouches nor the greenbacks. He had no idea how much had been in Hotchkiss's safe before the robbery, so it would not do much good to know how much he had recovered.

Nor did it bother him. In fact, as he started across the road to walk down to the liverybarn to see about arranging for gravediggers, it occurred to him that he would be secretly tickled if a sack or two were missing — just to watch Cal Hotchkiss squirm.

The corralyard-boss from up the road called out and came hurrying to reach Craig. There was a stranger with him, a young man with thick auburn hair dressed as a drover, perhaps as a freighter or coach-driver of some kind.

When the boss got up there, breathing slightly, he looked Craig squarely in the eye and said, "Marshal Stanton . . . meet Tobias White."

Craig smiled and extended a hand. "Right glad to meet you, Tobias."

He saw the odd look on the face of the corralyard boss, liked Tobias's smile and grip, freed his hand and turned. "What the hell's bothering you?" he asked the stage-company's local representative.

The boss squinted. "White, Marshal. Tobias *White . . .*"

Craig had overlooked it before. Now, he slowly returned his gaze to the young man. "Mind tellin' me your paw's name, Tobias?"

The drover offered a very faint, wistful

little smile. "I know what happened. I hadn't been in town twenty minutes off the morning stage and heard about it. . . . Marshal. . . . after twenty-five years, why did it happen last night when I was just a short distance and coming right along. Why — the very morning we would have met? Does that seem fair to you?"

Before Craig answered the corralyard-boss offered a feeble little wave and turned on his heel going back up the north walkway, and Craig watched his progress with detachment, then faced Tobias White and said, "I don't know. I'm just a town marshal."

He didn't *know,* and he never would *know,* but as he stood there with the anguished young man, he wondered what they could have talked about — how many horses did you steal, Paw? How much money did you make from stolen cattle? Or maybe old Jasper could have said, Your mother was a fine woman. Or, We missed having you along on the crossing — things which would not have meant a thing to each other. What could they possibly have discussed? What would both of them have felt, at first sight of each other — in a jailhouse?

"Had breakfast?" asked Craig a trifle gruffly, and when the young man nodded, he then said, "Well, walk along with me. I got to go down to the liverybarn for a few minutes."

As they turned to stride along Tobias White said, "Did he say anything to you, Marshal; mention he was thinkin' of killing himself?"

Craig sighed. "Not right out, no, he never mentioned it. Tobias, tell me one thing — how did you know he was down in this part of the country?"

"I didn't know it, Marshal. Last I knew, some fellers who knew my paw up at Deer Lodge in Montana said he used to talk about leaving the north country to go down along the south desert where a man wouldn't be forever freezing, so I started down the road. When I pulled into Cutler folks were talking." The young man watched someone down in front of the liverybarn bring out a handsome chestnut gelding and cross-tie him between a pair of trees in half sun, half shade, where he could get his back warmed and doze at the same time. "It just happened, Marshal, and it's still something I can't shake loose of — why, just overnight when we were this close, did he have to die?"

Craig took refuge in the presumed ignorance of frontiersmen. "I don't know. But he did, and now I got to bury him. And his partner, and an old man who got himself killed during the store robbery."

"My paw kill the old man?"

Craig could not give a forthright answer to that despite his innermost, secret convictions about it, which were not based on fact at all. "I don't know for a fact who killed him. It was dark and — well — you know how those things are. I expect folks will be debatin' that from now until the whole mess gets forgot about."

They paused out front of the barn. Craig smiled. "Wait here. I'll only be down there a few minutes."

He found the liveryman when he went looking for the dayman. "Need some graves dug," he announced and the vinegary liveryman responded sourly. "I expect you do. About three of them. Two deserve to go into the ground, by grabs."

Craig gazed up where the lean young man was standing out near that cross-tied horse and said, "Your hostlers be interested?"

"Damn right they will be, Marshal. I'd help dig *two* of them graves myself if I didn't have the rheumatics in my knees so bad."

"Tell 'em to see me at the jailhouse about noon," stated Marshal Stanton, still looking out where Tobias White was gazing up the roadway, studying the town.

The liveryman nodded. "I'll send them

up. By the way — who pays? Did them worthless bastards have some money on 'em? If they had it was probably stole somewhere." The liveryman let out a great sigh. "There's just gettin' to be too many people like that in the world, Marshal."

Craig walked back out into the sunlight, jerked his head and strolled thoughtfully northward in the direction of the jailhouse with young White beside him.

"You going to stay in town long?" he asked.

"No. When'll they bury him?"

"This evening. As soon as the holes are dug and I can round up the undertaker and preacher."

"It won't make much difference, will it? He's dead. He won't know I'm here."

"I guess he won't. But you found him, Tobias. Maybe it don't mean anything to him, now, but it might mean something to you — later on. To tell you the truth I don't know much about this sort of thing. Only . . . seems to me if I was in your boots, I'd be at the burying."

"What kind of a man did he seem to be, Marshal? Yeah, I know, an outlaw. But would there be more to him than that? I've got a little tintype photograph of them both when he was young. I think it was taken

181

just before they sold out to go west. My mother was a beautiful woman. She must have loved him. She must have had good judgment, Marshal."

Craig understood this to be a plea, and he swallowed hard before launching into his lie.

"Seemed like a brave man, Tobias. His partner was a lot younger than he was. Maybe his partner was a substitute for — someone else; maybe his son, I don't know. When I saw him, when we met south of here after the robbery, he looked tired. He'd sure earned the right to be that way. He was a — well — an average sort of man. I'd say your mother's judgment was good — back when she made it. When she died — it just took the heart out of him. I guess he was a decent-enough feller, except for his calling."

Craig turned to see how this had gone down. Tobias was expressionless as they arrived out front of the jailhouse and halted in shady warmth.

"Tobias, I got an idea about those fellers. Once they're dead, mistakes don't count. The truth is there, and you can't hide *that,* but hell, I never figured I was qualified to sit in judgment. Do you?"

The younger man raised grave eyes. "You

know, I wish you and my paw could have sat down and talked years back." He held out his hand and said, "Thanks, Marshal," then he walked up in the direction of the stage office.

Craig expected him to turn and buy passage on the next coach out of town. Instead, he trudged past and turned in at the tonsorial parlour. A man fixing to get shaved and shorn and sprinkled with toilet water, wasn't going to leave town. Not just yet anyway, which meant he would be at the burying.

Craig said, "Hell," and went briskly walking up toward the church.

He explained part of his reason why he wanted an elegant eulogy to the Methodist preacher, got a receptive response, then headed for the general store and when Cal came forward looking pithy and mildly hostile, Craig asked if he would be at the cemetery that evening. Cal's answer was clear. "Of course. Old Frank worked for me for twenty years and used to clerk for my paw afore that. But except for him I wouldn't spit on those other two graves."

Craig abandoned his usual tact. "Cal; don't you even *look* like you're going to open your mouth out there. You understand me? There's a young freighter or drover, or whatever he is, who's going to be out there too. Don't you even let him see how you feel."

"Why? What's a darned freighter to me?"

"This one is the son of Jasper White, the oldest of those outlaws."

Hotchkiss's eyes widened. "His son — here in Cutler? Marshal, I demand protection for my safe. I figured all along something like this would happen."

"No one's going to raid your damned safe, Cal. The lad is just passing through."

"Hmph! That's a likely story! He was probably in it up to his gullet, with his paw and that other bastard. You got no business lettin' a man like that walk the streets of this town. You'd ought to lock him —."

"Cal, shut up! Now you listen to me. The first feller who comes out there lookin' mean or makin' loose talk is goin' to get my boot right square in the butt as hard as I can kick. I'm warning you, Cal. After the funeral he's taking the stage on south. And you pass along the word. One smart remark out there and I'm going to wade in and do a little thinnin' out — startin' with you!"

Craig turned and stalked back out into the road and nearly collided with the town carpenter. He told him gruffly what he needed — three pine burying boxes and he needed them within the next hour or so.

The carpenter nodded. He always had an assortment of coffins in the back of his shop. There was little else to do in the long, bitter winters but make coffins.

Jeff Wayman and his riding crew turned into the main roadway from the northwest and Craig Stanton groaned, hitched at his belt and waited over in front of his jailhouse for them to see him and stop.

They had been going over to the cafe. They had left the ranch in the middle of the night and hadn't eaten since yesterday, but he intercepted them, said, "Good morning, gents," then asked how long they were going to be in town.

Jeff looked quizzically down. "All day. Why?"

"That old outlaw hanged himself in his cell last night."

The rangemen looked surprised.

"And his son came in on the morning coach. And we're going to bury the old bastard this evening." Craig smiled at them, one at a time. "If you boys aren't in town, fine. If you are, and if you get curious enough to mosey out and watch the burying — I'm askin' you to act decent. This feller never knew his paw."

"You mean," asked Cal Hamilton, "he don't know the old bastard was an outlaw?"

185

"Yeah, he knows that, but I been sort of tryin' to make his paw seem — well — not real terrible."

They sat their horses, stonily staring. Craig reddened a little. "Well; he never knew him, he's just here for today and will see him get buried. And the old cuss is dead, we got the money back —."

"But not my horses," stated Jeff flatly.

"In time, darn it," stated the lawman, his smile fading. "You expect everything done in one day?"

Luis Sanchez lightly rubbed the tip of his nose. "I understand," he told Craig. "*Simpatico,* eh?" Sanchez shrugged. "Yesterday I would have killed him. Today — he is dead." Sanchez shrugged again. "I understand."

But it was up to Jeff Wayman and he hung fire for a moment or two. It was impossible for a horse-rancher, whose main professional antagonism was toward people who stole horses, especially *his* horses, to shake all that hostility off in a moment.

He swung off and held the reins to his horse while gazing over in the direction of the cafe. Then he turned back and said, "Yeah. Well; we likely won't be in town that long. But all right — since the louse is dead — all right, Craig." He then turned to lead the way over to the rack out front of the

186

cafe and Craig entered the jailhouse one minute before the grave-diggers arrived, three liverybarn hostlers armed with shovels. One of them had a round, suspicious-looking bulge inside his old shirt which Craig ignored. If they thought digging was easier with whisky, more power to them.

He told them what he wanted and where to dig the graves, got rid of them and was going into the cell-room when the roadside door opened and the local undertaker arrived. Craig smiled with relief. "Where's your rig?" he asked, and when the undertaker jerked a thumb backwards the marshal said, "Take it around back into the alley. I'll carry him out there. And lay him out good, Jack. Comb his hair and all."

The undertaker looked pained. "What in hell for, he's only going into the ground."

"Because his son'll be there, that's why."

The undertaker stared. "His son?"

"Yeah. That's what I said — his darned son."

The undertaker shifted his cud of chewing tobacco. "To do all that will cost an extra two dollars, Craig."

"Five, if you make sure he's got a clean shirt on and all."

The undertaker held out a bony hand. Craig had to dig but he handed over the

crumpled greenback and after the undertaker had gone out to drive his rig around
back Craig called him a bad name.

15
"MARSHAL. . . ."

Like most men who had lived long enough
to wonder when things dovetailed so well,
Marshal Stanton was at his room over at
the boarding-house cleaning up, putting on
a fresh shirt and his Sunday boots when he
decided the preacher, the diggers, the
carpenter, had all done their work very well,
or were prepared to do it very well, and that
made him uneasy.

He knew a lot of people would be out
there. Not to see outlaws buried, and maybe
not entirely out of respect for old Frank,
but because they were curious.

He hung a new pair of gloves in his shellbelt, draped his church-going Prince Albert
coat over the gun, the gloves and shellbelt,
and went out into the late-day warmth and
hush.

The town was as quiet as it would have
been any Sunday morning. That added to
his unease as he struck out.

The cemetery was on the southeast side of town. It had some fairly old inhabitants out there; askew wooden boards barely decipherable any more. It also had a larger proportion of newer graves, almost exclusively marked by stones which would endure, probably longer than the town itself would last.

He had not seen Jasper's son since before noon, but when he reached the gate around the graveyard Tobias was standing over near an ancient oak tree, hair in place, boots greased, his face pale and solemn as he watched the same men who had dug the grave hoist his father's casket atop a pair of rickety old sawhorses.

He heard a sniffing sound among the motionless, clustered townsmen. Cal Hotchkiss was looking stonily at only one of those three pine boxes. He completely ignored the arrival of the marshal.

A lot more people were present than Craig had expected. Even Wayman and his Rafter W riding crew were on hand, in the discreet background since they were not dressed in black. The harness-maker was there, grim in the face, as was the paunchy liveryman, looking as impassive as possible as the preacher began his eulogy over old Frank first. It was fitting, and since a lot was known about old Frank, it was lengthy.

He even lingered to trickle in moist earth when they lowered Frank's coffin into the hole.

Jeff Wayman worked his way slowly and prudently up beside the town marshal and leaned slightly to whisper. "I know how he feels. I can see myself in him the day I had to go through this when my paw died."

Craig nodded mechanically as he watched the minister move to John Hall's box and begin a briefer but equally as eloquent a eulogy. Cal Hotchkiss started to turn, thin features showing contempt.

Craig eased over and halted directly behind the storekeeper. Their glances crossed and held. Hotchkiss reddened slightly and turned back.

The onlookers were stationary and at least a few of the women dabbed at their eyes from time to time, but the young man standing under the old tree near the final grave did not seem aware that there were people around him. He watched his father's partner get lowered by lass ropes, saw the men strain to retrieve their ropes, and reached, almost furtively, to briefly rest his hand upon the only coffin still atop its sawhorses. Craig saw; probably a lot of people saw, but the young man might as well have been the only one there.

The preacher moved along to the last coffin and as the perspiring diggers set their ropes for the lowering the preacher began speaking.

Craig was surprised. He was also proud of the minister. The eulogy was poignant, did not directly mention that the man behind him in the box had been an outlaw, but instead touched upon Jasper's life as a cowboy, as a wanderer among God's creatures. It asked forgiveness and made it sound as though the plea would have been the same for anyone.

Cal Hotchkiss muted his sniffing sound and Craig leaned to softly whisper. "Once more and I'm going to kick your butt."

They began lowering the coffin. The preacher scooped up dark earth and held it out to the young man, who took it and leaned to let it trickle downward. He had his back to them. There was not a sound except for the breath of the straining men on the lowering-ropes.

The minister lingered, Bible tucked under his arm as he stood beside the young man at graveside, his back to the silent throng. He softly said, "He will not be afraid, son. Believe in the miracle of forgiveness and peace. He will arise elsewhere a new man."

Craig felt a lump and over where Rafter W was standing Jeff seemed to be having a little trouble swallowing too. Then it was over as the lowering sun turned nearly scarlet above that sandstone cliff where Jasper and John had once camped; their last camp of solitude and peace, but no one knew it.

Craig stepped away so that Hotchkiss could finally walk away. They exchanged a look. Cal's scornful expression was gone. He nodded and Craig nodded back.

Jeff Wayman took his riders with him amid the dispersing throng of townsmen. The preacher walked back to town beside his diminutive, dark-eyed wife leaving only Craig and Tobias White.

The young man did not move for a long while, but when he finally turned and saw the marshal back there, like stone, he hitched at his shoulders and walked back.

"Thanks," he said, shoving out a hand, and afterwards he fished in a pocket. "Something I'd like to show you." It was a deputy U.S. marshal's badge. Craig stared at it, slowly raised his eyes and said, "You weren't after *him,* were you?"

Tobias White dropped the badge back into its pocket. "Not in the way you mean, no. But that was my assignment. Marshal; do you reckon that was why I wasn't supposed to find him alive?"

All Craig could think of right at the moment was how awful it would have been if the son had indeed found his father alive. How agonising for them both.

"Right now, Mister White, I'd say it sure looks to me like you weren't supposed to find him alive. I'll walk you back to the stage office."

Little was said until they reached the plankwalk and walked up it to the corral-yard gate where the evening stage was being loaded and the deputy U.S. marshal smiled. Craig Stanton asked the uppermost question in his mind. "If you had found him alive . . . ?"

Tobias's smile faded. "I can't answer that. I've been trying for a couple of months, ever since I started looking for him. I've been a deputy marshal for two years. I like the work and I didn't know him, hadn't seen him since I was too young to remember. . . . How thick is blood, Marshal Stanton?"

Craig nodded his head as they wheeled the stage out front for the passengers. "Good luck," he said. "Any time you come through, I'll walk out there with you."

Craig turned to slow-pace down in the direction of the jailhouse. Normally, he would have gone back to his room to change. This early evening he didn't care whether he changed or not, he had a knotty problem to think about. He would never find the answer to it, and presumably, neither would Deputy U.S. Marshal Tobias White.

We hope you have enjoyed this Large Print book. Other Thorndike, Wheeler, Kennebec, and Chivers Press Large Print books are available at your library or directly from the publishers.

For information about current and upcoming titles, please call or write, without obligation, to:

Publisher
Thorndike Press
10 Water St., Suite 310
Waterville, ME 04901
Tel. (800) 223-1244

or visit our Web site at:

http://gale.cengage.com/thorndike

OR

Chivers Large Print
published by AudioGO Ltd
St James House, The Square
Lower Bristol Road
Bath BA2 3SB
England
Tel. +44(0) 800 136919
email: info@audiogo.co.uk
www.audiogo.co.uk

All our Large Print titles are designed for easy reading, and all our books are made to last.